THE CRYPTID CATCHER

Lija Fisher

THE CRYPTID CATCHER

SQUARE
FISH

Farrar Straus Giroux
New York

SQUARE
FISH

An imprint of Macmillan Publishing Group, LLC
120 Broadway, New York, NY 10271
mackids.com

Our books may be purchased in bulk for promotional, educational, or business
use. Please contact your local bookseller or the Macmillan Corporate and
Premium Sales Department at (800) 221-7945 ext. 5442 or by email at
MacmillanSpecialMarkets@macmillan.com.

Library of Congress Cataloging-in-Publication Data

Names: Fisher, Lija, author.
Title: The cryptid catcher / Lija Fisher.
Description: New York : Farrar Straus Giroux, 2018. | Summary:
  Thirteen-year-old Clivo Wren learns that his recently deceased father
  was not an archaeologist as he was told, but rather a cryptid catcher,
  known for finding elusive mythological creatures, and now Clivo must
  pick up where his father left off and track down a cryptid whose blood
  grants immortality before the knowledge falls into the wrong hands.
Identifiers: LCCN 2017042496 | ISBN 978-1-250-30852-8 (paperback) |
  ISBN 978-0-374-30555-0 (ebook)
Subjects: | CYAC: Animals, Mythical—Fiction. | Secret societies—Fiction. |
  Adventure and adventurers—Fiction.
Classification: LCC PZ7.1.F5684 Cr 2018 | DDC [Fic]—dc23
LC record available at https://lccn.loc.gov/2017042496

Originally published in the United States by Farrar Straus Giroux
First Square Fish edition, 2019
Book designed by Aimee Fleck
Square Fish logo designed by Filomena Tuosto

1   3   5   7   9   10   8   6   4   2

AR: 5.8 / LEXILE: 850L

*To those who live their lives believing
that someday a door will open, a hand will reach
through to beckon, and a voice will whisper,
"Come. Your adventure awaits."*

THE CRYPTID CATCHER

Prologue

Russell Wren ducked away from the chupacabra paw that swung uncomfortably close to his face, the razor-sharp tip of a claw just barely scratching his cheek.

"Whoa! Easy, guy! I'm just trying to talk to you!" Russell exclaimed. He had encountered a lot of angry beasts, but the chupacabra seemed to be particularly prickly.

The creature rose up on its hind legs and began punching at Russell like a boxer, forcing him to dodge and deflect blow after blow.

"Will you please just calm down?" Russell begged as a paw caught him squarely in the cheek, causing him to see stars.

The rain fell in a light mist around him, making it difficult to keep his footing on the slick moss and roots that covered the floor of the Colombian tropical forest. The chupacabra was actually less scary than Russell had been expecting. Many sightings of the legendary "goatsucker" claimed it had spikes on its back and fangs as long as tusks. But in reality, it was just a massive, mangy-looking, doglike cryptid with gray fur that was able to hop around like a kangaroo.

Russell blocked another punch from the creature and quickly swept his leg underneath it, knocking it to the ground. The chupacabra let out a whine and Russell scrambled to his tranquilizer gun, which had been flung aside earlier in the fight. Just as his hand closed on the barrel, something sharp and metallic hit the weapon, sending up a shower of sparks.

"Holy *demon dog*!"

Russell whirled around just as the beast lifted its paw and shot another detachable claw directly at him. Russell had just enough time to bring up his gun and deflect the lethal projectile to the ground.

"Okay, buddy, this has gone way too far," Russell complained. He smoothly aimed his gun and fired, the dart easily finding its mark.

The chupacabra let out another whine and rolled onto its back, its paws clawing at the dart, its limbs slowly going limp as the tranquilizer took effect.

Russell hurried over and gently removed the dart, rubbing the wound to help relieve the sting. "It's okay, buddy. I'm not going to hurt you. I just need to check something; then I'll leave you alone, I promise."

Russell stroked the wiry hair of the creature, talking quietly to it as it slowly slipped into unconsciousness. When it was fully asleep, Russell let out an exhausted sigh. "I am definitely getting too old for this," he mumbled.

He pulled out a small cylindrical device and took a sample of the creature's blood, waiting in anticipation as the device beeped. Russell held his breath, hoping with all his being that he had finally found the treasure he was searching for, but when a few words popped up on the device's small screen, he growled in frustration. He ran his hands through his sandy-blond hair in exasperation and scratched the five-day-old beard that had grown during the time he had waited in the jungle, tracking the chupacabra.

He had been so sure this was the one, that his search, which had spanned decades, would finally be over—his search for the greatest secret known to man, held by a creature that should not exist. A secret that in the wrong hands could mean the end of humanity as he knew it.

Alas, his quest would have to continue.

Russell pulled himself together and patted the creature gently. "Sorry, guy, you're not the beast I am looking for."

He packed away his device, took his usual smiling selfie with the creature even though he wasn't feeling that cheerful, and began his long trek out of the lush forest. The chupacabra would wake up soon, and Russell wanted to be as far away from those sharp claws as possible.

On his journey back, Russell wondered what he was doing wrong. He'd been searching for the one special mythological beast for years—the cryptid whose blood contained the secret to life everlasting. Why hadn't he found it? He was a good tracker, he had the best research team on his side, but still the creature remained a mystery.

At first Russell had enjoyed the search. The excitement, the adrenaline, the thrill of discovering creatures that weren't supposed to exist. But his quest had become more pressing. More people were looking for the One—dangerous people, people who would use the secret to rule the world. Russell was the only cryptid catcher who sought to protect the creature, to make sure its treasure remained safe from those who would use it for evil. But with a gathering group of villains on the hunt, time was running out.

After hours of trekking through the lush, canopied forest—which would have been pleasant save for the persistent rain that soaked his cargo pants through—he finally made it to his jeep. As he scrambled for his keys, he thought of his son waiting for him at home, and he smiled. Someday, hopefully soon, he could spend all of his time with him without running off every few months to go on another hunt. But he had to find the creature first, to protect his family—and the world.

Russell had opened the door to his jeep and was about to climb inside when a noise sounded behind him. Maybe it was the fatigue, or distraction from the frustrations of the hunt, but he hadn't sensed the danger around him. He turned and had just a moment to think about his son one final time before all went black.

Sunday

I

The rickety Pinto turned the corner and sputtered toward Jerry's house, backfiring loudly like a fireworks finale. From the front porch, Clivo and Jerry watched the car motor toward them, and Clivo swallowed. He wasn't sure he was ready for this.

"You ready for this?" Jerry asked.

"Would you be?" Clivo sighed.

Jerry gave him a sympathetic pat on the back. "Better you than me."

Clivo guffawed. "Thanks."

It was finally time for Clivo Wren to go home, though he wasn't looking forward to it. After his father died earlier in the summer, he'd moved in with Jerry, his best friend, and Jerry's parents in their spacious home in Old Colorado City. The place was comfortable and everyone did their best to help him feel at home. Jerry had kept playing his usual pranks, which made Clivo laugh, to help keep Clivo's mind off the fact that he had just become an orphan.

"You can keep staying with us, you know," Jerry said,

glancing at Clivo. "And it's not just a pity party 'cause you've reached orphan status, either. I think having you around to mess with has been super fun."

Clivo winced as the car backfired again. "I think you want to keep me around 'cause it gives your mom someone else to smother."

Jerry flashed his wide smile. "That's part of it."

Clivo laughed. "I want to stay, trust me. But I don't want to hurt Aunt Pearl's feelings, since she's willing to be my guardian and all. Plus, school starts tomorrow."

"Your loss." Jerry shrugged.

Jerry Cooper had inherited most of his father's dark African American skin tone, even though Mrs. Cooper was as pale as a cave dweller. When Jerry was younger, the other moms at the playground had thought Mrs. Cooper was Jerry's nanny, which she used to her advantage with her son. Whenever Jerry started raising a ruckus, she'd say that if he didn't behave she could easily disown him because nobody believed he belonged to her anyway. Unfortunately, not even the threat of maternal abandonment caused Jerry to behave.

"Here she comes!" Mrs. Cooper exclaimed, waddling out the front door. She was short and shaped like a turnip, but had enough spunk in her to launch a rocket ship. "You ready for this, honey?"

"I'm ready," Clivo said, forcing a smile. He adjusted the bag on his shoulder and watched the Pinto get even closer, the glittery ANIMALS ON BOARD! sticker flashing on the front bumper like an evil smile.

Mr. Cooper followed Mrs. Cooper onto the porch. "Oops, oops, I almost missed the goodbyes! Wait for me, son, don't hightail it out of here just yet!"

Mr. Cooper looked just like Jerry, save for a potbelly, a receding hairline, and a pair of glasses that made his eyeballs look three times as big. So actually he looked nothing like Jerry, who spent half an hour in front of the mirror every morning making sure his hairdo could withstand the wind from a tornado.

"You ready for this, son?" Mr. Cooper asked, giving Clivo's shoulder a squeeze.

Clivo groaned inwardly. The last thing in the world he wanted was to get in that Pinto. "I'm ready, Mr. Cooper."

The Pinto came to a stop in front of them, the brakes squealing. Clivo winced.

His aunt tooted the horn and waved and smiled, but made no effort to get out of the vehicle.

"Good luck," Jerry said, saluting as if Clivo were going off to war.

"If you don't hear from me in three days, send help," Clivo replied, half-heartedly returning the gesture.

"You sure you don't want to borrow my football helmet?" Jerry asked, his face wrinkling with concern. "A little protection wouldn't hurt, you know."

"Actually, could I? It'd probably help."

"I was kidding! I don't need your head lice in my equipment."

Clivo sighed again and grabbed his bags slowly, as if they weighed a hundred pounds. He did kind of feel like he was going off to battle.

"Take care, son," Mr. Cooper said, giving Clivo a big hug.

"Thank you, Mr. and Mrs. Cooper, for everything you've done for me over the past month. Living with you has been really great."

Mrs. Cooper wiped a tear from her eye and grabbed Clivo's dimpled cheeks. "The house will be empty without you here."

Jerry cleared his throat. "You know that I'll still be around, right, Ma?"

"Oh, you know I love you more than life itself. But your bro from another schmo tickles my heart, too."

"It's 'brother from another mother,' Ma! How hard is that to remember?" Jerry lectured.

Clivo reluctantly turned away from the place he had been calling home and walked as slowly as possible toward the Pinto, his feet dragging in protest. The car was a cheery yellow, but he knew what horrors were inside. He paused in front of the rear window and looked at his reflection. Nothing had changed in his appearance during the four weeks he had been with the Coopers. His brown hair was still a shaggy mess and his clothes were still woefully out of style. Aunt Pearl had been the one who always took him shopping when she came to visit, and she thought anything on the dollar rack at Palace of Pants was fashionable.

He looked at the worn beaded bracelet on his wrist, having almost forgotten he still wore it. It was a Tibetan Buddhist bracelet his dad had given him after one of his overseas archaeological digs. Clivo had begun wearing it shortly after the funeral, just to feel close to his dad again. He knew that didn't make sense, since they had never been that close to begin with. Still, he hadn't been able to bring himself to take it off. It reminded him that, at one point at least, he had had a family of his own.

Mr. Cooper coughed behind him. "I don't think the trunk opens itself, son."

Mrs. Cooper shushed her husband. "Give him a minute! He needs to process!"

Clivo shook himself out of his thoughts, opened the Pinto's hatchback, and tossed in his bags.

"Hello, Clivo!" his aunt said from the front seat, her bright eyes looking at him in the mirror. "Watch out for my creatures. They insisted on coming to get you."

"Hi, Aunt Pearl!" Clivo said, shutting the hatch carefully.

He went to the passenger side of the car and braced himself before climbing in as quickly as possible, closing his eyes and holding his breath in preparation. Within moments of his taking a seat, a purring pair of long-haired cats slithered from his aunt's lap like a slo-mo Navy SEAL team on a mission and wrapped themselves tightly around Clivo's neck and shoulders.

"Argh!" Clivo exclaimed, desperately trying to get to his seat belt without inhaling a pound of fur.

From the front porch, Jerry shook his head in sympathy.

"Why didn't you offer him your football helmet?" Mrs. Cooper chided her son as they headed back inside the house. "He needed some protection!"

"I tried, Ma!"

Clivo and Aunt Pearl headed west into the Rockies from Old Colorado City and soon were winding their way up the familiar paved and then dirt roads, the hot August air getting cooler as they climbed in altitude. Aunt Pearl's tanned hands tapped rhythmically on the steering wheel, as if she were discreetly playing the bongos.

After his father's funeral, Clivo's aunt had agreed to give up her apartment in town and move to Clivo's isolated mountainside home with her two horrible cats after she returned from a "holy church pilgrimage," which was really just a monthlong vacation with her salsa-dancing group at a tropical resort in Acapulco.

Pearl had once been a purehearted churchgoing lady who accidentally wandered into the wrong meeting room in her church basement one day and found herself in a salsa-dancing class instead of a prayer group; now she snuck off as frequently as possible to indulge in her secret passion.

"Did you have a nice visit with your friend Jeff, sweetheart?" Aunt Pearl asked with a smile. She had tightly curled mouse-colored hair and was tall and thin, like a stork, with a nose like a long beak. Her plain dress made her look like a quiet, bookish type—so much so that Clivo had a hard time picturing her tearing up the dance floor.

"Um, with Jerry?" Clivo gently corrected.

To say that Aunt Pearl was absentminded was an understatement. She had done her best at raising him whenever his dad was away on one of his frequent work trips, but more often than not she had forgotten that Clivo was even around. He had spent more afternoons than he could count sitting in the principal's office because Aunt Pearl had forgotten to pick him up from school, even though she had dropped him off that morning.

"Yeah, Aunt Pearl, it was a good break. How was your pilgrimage?"

"Oh, it was absolutely heaven," Aunt Pearl said with a contented sigh, her fingers picking up their rhythmic tapping on the steering wheel. "Oh, before I forget, there's a present for you in the back seat. I know I missed your birthday in June, but I still wanted to get you a little something."

"Thanks, Aunt Pearl," Clivo said, tearing the wrapped

gift away from a cat who was chewing on the ribbon. "My birthday was actually this month, August, but . . ."

"Has it always been in August?" Aunt Pearl asked with a confused expression.

"Ever since I was born in August," Clivo replied with a shrug.

Aunt Pearl giggled and pinched his cheek. "You are such a little rascal!"

Clivo shook his head and unwrapped the gift, revealing a white stuffed Pegasus with golden wings. The cats immediately began hissing at it.

"Wow, a Pegasus. That's great, Aunt Pearl. Thank you," Clivo said, trying to keep the disappointment out of his voice.

"Aw, you're welcome, sweetie. I know how much you love cuddling with your stuftees," she replied, giving his leg a loving pat.

Clivo winced. No matter how old he got, Aunt Pearl insisted on talking to him as if he were a baby. "I did, definitely, but I'm a teenager now, so I probably won't be needing more stuffed animals. I mean, this one is great, thank you, but I'll probably be growing out of them soon." Clivo didn't want to hurt his aunt's feelings, but he also didn't want to spend the rest of his life collecting stuffed animals.

"A teenager?" Aunt Pearl asked, her face taking on its confused, glazed expression, one that Clivo saw a lot. "When did you turn thirteen?"

"Um, on my birthday?"

"The one in April?" Aunt Pearl asked.

"That would be the one," Clivo replied, giving up on trying to correct her.

Aunt Pearl's face melted into a joyous smile and she once again pinched his cheek. "My little rascal is a little man now!"

Half an hour later, they pulled up the long gravel driveway to the isolated two-story craftsman-style bungalow that was his real home, although the Coopers' house had felt more comfortable than this place had in years.

"Welcome home, sweetheart," Aunt Pearl said, her fingers pausing their drumming. "The kitties and I moved our things in yesterday so we'd be all set for your arrival."

Clivo sat in the car with two cats curled on his shoulders and stared at his empty childhood home. The place looked foreign and deserted. Dead leaves gathered on the ground and faded green paint peeled from the trim. A sagging teepee his father had made from animal skins stood in the yard and a wooden statue that looked like a carved head from Easter Island sat on the porch, chipped paint gathering at its base. Chinese wind-bells dangled from the eaves, letting out a tinkling that was supposed to ward off evil spirits, though Clivo thought they must not work very well if the cats had been allowed in the house. Strewn throughout the yard were other tattered mementos from his dad's trips—Japanese water fountains, Tibetan prayer flags, and embarrassing Polynesian sculptures of naked people that Aunt Pearl seemed to have clothed in sweat-shirts and skirts.

"You excited to be back home, sweetie?" Aunt Pearl asked nervously. "I cleaned the place up nicely for you. And the cats already love sleeping in your room; I hope you don't mind."

Clivo winced at that. The wind-bells definitely didn't work.

"Yeah, it's nice to be home," Clivo agreed, though that wasn't at all how he felt as he stared at the dark windows.

After helping his aunt bring the cats inside, Clivo emptied the car and took his bags up to his room, which smelled like felines. When he went downstairs he found his aunt and the cats waiting for him in the living room.

"So, um, I made some mac and cheese for you. It's on the stove," Pearl continued. "I'd eat with you tonight, but there's a special Bible-study class going on at church. Would you mind if I went?"

Clivo knew by now that "going to church" meant "going out dancing." He'd even noticed that peeking out from under Aunt Pearl's conservative black skirt was the brightly colored hem of her dancing outfit.

"That's fine, Aunt Pearl," Clivo said. He didn't really want to spend the evening alone in the empty house, but

Pearl would probably just make him sit quietly next to her and play with his new stuffed animal all night, anyway. "You go have fun at church."

Pearl's face burst into a grin. "Okay, thanks, sweetheart. Please remember to feed the kitties their dinner. Not too much or they'll use your bed as a litter box! And give them some good scratchies underneath their chinny chin chins!"

Wasting no time, she hustled out the door. A few moments later, she fired up the Pinto and took off, the car's spinning tires spattering gravel against the front door.

"Come on, guys!" Clivo moaned as the cats crowded around him. "Ricky Martin, out of my way. You, too, Julio Iglesias. If you nip me one more time I'm throwing you to the coyotes."

Clivo turned on a few of the antique lamps with stained-glass shades to brighten up the place. The house was so sheltered by the surrounding pine trees that even in the middle of the day it could be as dark as a cave. And with all the artifacts from his dad's trips, the house looked like an old museum. A zebra head hung on one wall, a didgeridoo leaned against a corner, and a brass incense burner dangled from a chain. The house smelled like flowery dust—Pearl must have spritzed some of her drugstore perfume around to cover up the antique smell of the place.

This weird house high up in the mountains, away from everything and everyone, was the only home Clivo had ever known. It was a part of who he was, yet he sometimes wished he'd grown up in a nice suburban house surrounded by neighbors, with grass and not forest for a yard.

"Hey, Bernie," Clivo said, knocking on the suit of armor that stood in the corner. Bernie was now wearing a checkered apron; apparently Aunt Pearl thought that even a naked suit of armor was indecent.

Clivo warmed up the pasta, spooned himself a bowlful, locked the protesting cats in the kitchen with their food, and made himself comfortable on the couch. He turned the TV on and immediately grunted in frustration when he realized the cable service had been turned off. No doubt the latest bill hadn't been paid. So Clivo sat in silence in the dark house, his mind drifting to how much he missed his parents. He didn't remember much about his mom because she'd gotten sick and died when he was only five, but if he really concentrated he could just hear her soothing voice reading him bedtime stories every night, followed by the tinkling of an old Egyptian rattle that she'd jangled over his head to protect him from the God of Storms. Clivo wished she had used a rattle to protect him from the god that stole parents, if there was such a thing.

II

A sharp knock on the front door jerked Clivo from sleep. He froze. Nobody ever visited their house. A moment later, an even sharper knock sounded, so loudly it seemed like part of the wooden door had splintered.

Clivo slowly opened the door just as a bolt of lightning and a crack of thunder hit. While he had been napping, the sun had set and a storm had rolled in, pouring sheets of rain onto the gravel driveway. The flash of lightning illuminated a stout old man with wild gray hair and a gold cane.

"You Clivo Wren?" the figure asked in a gruff voice.

"Um, yeah," Clivo replied hesitantly.

"You know who I am, kid?"

Clivo looked closer, trying to see if anything about the old man with a bulbous red nose and a nice wool jacket rang a bell.

"I don't think so," Clivo finally replied.

"Either you do or you don't. Now let me in; it's wetter than a whale's rear out here," the man said, trying to push Clivo aside with his cane.

Clivo held his ground.

"Sorry, no strangers in the house."

The old man sighed and looked up at the sky.

"Don't tell me he's a brat. Please don't tell me Russell raised a brat."

This made Clivo relax.

"You knew Russell?"

The man pulled out a handkerchief and coughed violently into it. Once he recovered he spoke again, his voice strained from the coughing.

"Knew him? I hired him. My card."

The man pulled a small case from his jacket and produced a card. It was made of thin silver, almost like tinfoil, with two simple words engraved on it: DOUGLAS CHANCERY.

Clivo flipped the card over, but the rest was blank.

"Are you a spy?" Clivo asked.

That just about sent Douglas into another coughing fit.

"A spy?" Douglas sputtered. "Do I look like James Bond to you?"

"Well, I thought that business cards were supposed to tell how to reach you in order to, you know, do business," Clivo replied.

"I know you kids are used to Facetwitting all the time, but it used to be that one had a bit of privacy in this world. Now let me in before I drown out here or get electrocuted."

Clivo raised his eyebrows and let the man pass.

Douglas hobbled into the house and stood in the foyer.

"Ah, nice place. Oddly decorated, although your dad always was a bit of a magic cookie."

Douglas solidly smacked Bernie a few times with his cane, leaving a dent in the armor.

"What can I do for you, Mr. Chancery?" Clivo asked, stepping protectively in front of his metal friend.

"One thing, pronto: scotch, neat. And give me a strong pour. I've been drinking longer than you've had hair on your head, so don't shortchange me."

Clivo raised his eyebrows again but kept his mouth shut as he headed toward the kitchen. His mom had taught him to respect his elders, although this guy was really pushing it.

"But first take my jacket! Were you raised by wolves?" Douglas yelled after him.

Clivo mumbled to himself that he'd like to throw Mr. Chancery to the wolves but went back and took the jacket. By the time he turned from the hall closet, Douglas was already in the den, sifting through the books on the shelves.

Russell's study was just what you would expect for an obsessive archaeologist. Old maps hung on the walls, a dusty globe sat in one corner, overflowing bookcases lined one entire wall, and two cushy chairs sat side by side with a small table bearing an ashtray in between. The room smelled of pungent Colombian mocha tobacco smoke from his dad's pipe, which was still propped on the large mahogany desk.

Clivo went to the kitchen and filled a pint glass with soda and ice cubes. He returned to the den and handed Douglas the drink.

"What the heck is this?" Douglas bellowed.

"Ginger ale. We don't have any alcohol in the house. Aunt Pearl says drinking it only leads to tomfoolery, whatever that means."

"For the record, I enjoy being led into tomfoolery." Douglas fished the ice cubes from his glass and placed them in the hands of a Hindu goddess statue. He took a flask out of his jacket pocket and poured some amber liquid into his drink before taking a hearty swig. "Ah, much better."

Douglas eased his body down into what had been Russell's chair. Clivo tensed; he didn't like this gruff man sitting in his father's seat.

"Any chance you've got some crackers and caviar?" Douglas asked.

"How about saltines and Cheez Whiz?" Clivo mumbled. He picked up the ice cubes and threw them into a plant.

"Hah! Nice comeback. Brats I can't stand, but witty snarks I can handle. It makes sense that Russell raised a smart kid; he always struck me as being the 'loving father' type." Douglas said the last bit as if it were a bad thing.

"I guess so; he just wasn't around that much."

"Oh, yes, boo-hoo. Daddy's not here to teach me how to catch a football or wear cologne. That's the problem with kids—they get in the way of all the important stuff. Little narcissists are what they are." Douglas inhaled another swig of his drink.

"Mr. Chancery, can you please tell me what you're doing here?" Clivo was still standing. He didn't know who this man was, and something about him made Clivo's spine tingle with foreboding.

Douglas sat forward eagerly in his chair, a twinkle in his eye from excitement (or the drink). Setting his glass on the table, he rubbed his hands together quickly, as if he were rubbing two sticks to start a fire.

"Get ready to have your mind blown, kid," he said.

Clivo remained where he was, warily looking at the stranger. This was obviously not the reaction Douglas had hoped for, because he impatiently cleared his throat.

"Usually when someone tells you you're about to have your mind blown, you give them the courtesy of sitting down."

"I can have my mind blown just fine while standing up," Clivo replied, keeping his distance.

Douglas glared at him.

"Your snark, although initially charming, is now tip-toeing too close to bratsville." Douglas slapped the armrest and sat back in a pout. "Now you've ruined the moment. It's totally gone. And there was such a nice buildup to it, too."

Clivo let out a sigh. The man seemed too old to be of any real danger, so Clivo went back to the kitchen and grabbed a ginger ale for himself. He returned to the den and reluctantly took a seat next to Douglas.

"All right, Mr. Chancery, my mind is prepared to be blown."

That seemed to put Douglas back in the mood again. He leaned forward in his chair and peered at Clivo with his bloodshot eyes. He spoke the next words slowly and deliberately.

"Kid, your father was not an archaeologist. He was a cryptid catcher."

Douglas took a sip of his drink as he eagerly awaited Clivo's reaction, which was one of utter confusion. "He was a who?"

"Ha! That got your attention!" Douglas exclaimed, getting up and pacing around the room. "A cryptid catcher. A hunter of mythological creatures. A stalker of legends. A pursuer of parables, a fisherman of fables. You know, a cryptid catcher."

"Repeating the same strange phrase doesn't really make me understand it any better," Clivo said.

"Oh, right," Douglas said, retaking his seat. "What was the question again?"

"I don't have a question!" Clivo replied loudly. "Russell was an archaeologist. With a focus on medieval and colonial archaeology—"

"Yep, I recommended the medieval and colonial bit. It's an easy cover for flying all over the world. And why do you call him Russell instead of Dad or 'my dear father'? I've never heard a kid call their father by his first name."

Clivo ignored the question and chugged his soda. The man wasn't dangerous, but he was obviously off his rocker. As much as Clivo didn't want to be alone, being stuck for the evening with this man seemed even worse.

He reached for Douglas's nearly empty glass. "If you've finished your drink—"

Douglas jerked his glass out of Clivo's reach. "I am certainly *not* done with my drink, nor are we done with this conversation. And I must say, I am extremely disappointed in your lack of shock and awe at what I've just told you."

"Mr. Chancery, you walk in here, a total stranger, and tell me that my dad hunted unicorns. Wouldn't you ask yourself to leave?"

Douglas waved his hand dismissively. "Not unicorns, haven't found one of those yet. And he didn't hunt them. He caught them. Don't start spreading rumors that your dad was a poacher; he had far too strong a moral compass for that."

Clivo shook his head in confusion and stood up. "All right, Mr. Chancery, it's past my bedtime so I should probably . . ."

Douglas stood up with a grunt of exertion, but instead of leaving, he walked around the room, poking the tip of his cane at the spines of the tomes on the bookshelves.

"Did your father read to you as a child?" Douglas finally asked. Clivo threw his arms up in exasperation. Douglas ignored him. "Regular kiddie books or . . . other stuff?"

Clivo sighed. "Um, I don't know what other kids had read to them, but I guess other stuff. The front door is this way, Mr. Chancery."

Douglas went back to scanning the bookshelves. If the old man insisted on staying much longer, Clivo thought, he would be forced to call the police. Or Jerry. Jerry could probably pick the guy up and fling him over his shoulder, no problem, or at the very least give him a good tackle.

Finally Douglas found what he was looking for. He pulled out a book and handed it to Clivo.

"Did he ever read you this?"

That made Clivo pause. He didn't even have to look at the title; he knew from the faded green fabric cover and dark-brown leather binding that it was a translation of *Les*

Propheties, a book of prophecies by the French apothecary and seer Nostradamus published in the sixteenth century.

"Yeah, we read it sometimes. We'd play a game where he'd read a prophecy and I'd have to figure out what it meant," Clivo said, his hands cupping the familiar book with ease.

"Read page two eighty-eight, in the 'Lost Verses' section," Douglas said, his eyes still sorting through the books.

Clivo muttered to himself but found the spot, turning the old pages with delicacy. He read the prophecy aloud.

"All creatures, one blood. Some remain hidden, others come fore. In one who is hidden, the blood is gone, replaced by the spring of life. A silver lightning drop of eternity."

"And what did you determine that prophecy to mean?" Douglas asked, his voice a dramatic whisper.

"I don't think we ever read that one," Clivo replied.

"Oh," Douglas said, disappointed. "Well, now that you have, what do you think the prophecy means?"

Clivo scratched his head.

"I don't know. I mean, it kinda sounds like there's a creature out there that's immortal."

"That's right, kid, that's exactly right!" Douglas said, practically dancing back to his chair and sitting down. "There's a cryptid out there whose body is filled not with ordinary blood, but with a special type that, we think, makes it, and could make us . . . immortal." Douglas drew out the last word with as much dramatic aplomb as possible.

Clivo put the book back. He had heard enough tall tales for one night.

"That's fascinating, Mr. Chancery, and maybe we can talk about it some other time when it's not so late."

And bring Bigfoot along with you, Clivo thought wryly.

Douglas swallowed the rest of his drink and stood up with a grunt. His tart breath assaulted Clivo's nose as he brought his face uncomfortably close.

"I'll cut to the chase, kid, since you obviously don't have a flair for the dramatic. Your father was a cryptid catcher, the best one out there. He was searching for the immortal cryptid to ensure that it didn't fall into the wrong hands. He tried to find it before your mom died so he could save her from her illness, which would have been a big no-no, but I guess love makes you do stupid things, which is why I avoid it at all costs. Anyhow, he wanted you to follow in his footsteps, but he was killed by a chupacabra before he could reveal everything to you on your eighteenth birthday."

Clivo balked. "My father was killed by a landslide in Puerto Rico while digging at the Caparra Archaeological Site. Not by a mythological creature."

Douglas's eyes narrowed. "The Caparra Archaeological Site, location of the first Spanish capital on the island, founded in 1508 and abandoned thirteen years later, after the area kept getting attacked by the locals, was declared a U.S. historic landmark in 1994. It's illegal for private archaeologists to dig there, so it's not possible your dad was there. Russell was the best cryptid catcher, but not always the best liar." Douglas pulled a wrinkled piece of paper from his chest pocket. "So, thanks to his demise, I now have to hire you. Very reluctantly, of course. I don't trust people who aren't old enough to grow facial hair. But your dad made me sign a stupid contract. Once he realized he was darned good at this catching thing, he made me agree to only hire him or you. Apparently he had seen some stuff in the field that made him not trust anyone else with the task of finding the immortal. He worried that even the stoutest-hearted individual would turn evil with such power in their hands. But not you. He trusted you—why, I have no idea; that scrappy hair of yours makes you look like a derelict, in my book."

Curious, Clivo took the wrinkled piece of paper and unfolded it. It was covered with what must have been Douglas's sloppy handwriting.

I, Douglas Chancery, agree that I will only hire Russell Wren or his son, Clivo Wren (which is stupid because he's an infant right now and doesn't even know what his hand is, much less a cryptid). Still, due to Russell's incredibly good ability to catch beasts, I will trust him to train his son to take after him. In turn, Russell guarantees me that his son will not be a ruffian and will actually be good at catching (something I highly doubt right now since he just pooped his shorts), or else I can fire his stinky butt if and when I feel like it.

At the bottom of the page were Douglas's and Russell's signatures, next to a baby's tiny footprint in black ink.

"And I suppose you're going to tell me that's my footprint?" Clivo asked, giving Douglas back the paper.

"Yep. You were the only witness to this transaction, so we needed your signature to make it legal and binding."

Clivo rolled his eyes and walked to the hall closet, where he got Douglas's coat. "There's just one thing wrong with your story, sir."

"Enlighten me," Douglas growled, struggling into his heavy jacket.

"That my dad cared enough to want me to follow in his footsteps. He got away from me every chance he got."

"You kids are so needy nowadays," Douglas spat. "Daddy—excuse me—*Russell* was off saving the world, and the only thing you were concerned about was that he wasn't there to watch your boring T-ball game. You probably didn't even notice all the time he spent training you."

"What training?" Clivo asked, turning his back on Douglas to open the front door.

The next few seconds went by in a blur. Douglas suddenly swung his cane at Clivo's head. Instinctually Clivo blocked the stick with his left forearm. Next Douglas's left fist came at him, which Clivo deflected as well. But Douglas wasn't done; his left leg swept under Clivo's feet, knocking him onto his back. In half a second, Clivo tucked his legs underneath him and sprang back to standing, one hand grabbing Douglas loosely but threateningly by the throat.

Douglas smiled with satisfaction. "*That* training. Let me guess, martial arts classes since you were, what, three or four?"

"Two and a half," Clivo said, his breath coming in gasps, both from exertion and adrenaline. The man had just *attacked* him!

"None of that karate crap, I hope."

"Jujitsu," Clivo said, confusion coursing through his mind.

"Archery?"

"Starting age five."

"Shooting?"

"Six."

"Survival skills?"

"Like going winter camping in subzero temperatures? Age seven."

"Languages?"

"Five. Japanese, Hindustani, Arabic, Russian. And English."

"Hindustani?" Douglas asked with disgust. "Well, I'm sure Russell had a reason for it. I learned long ago never to ask him his reasons for things. If something ain't broke, don't fix it." Douglas carefully removed Clivo's shaking hand from his throat. "And I suppose you never wondered why your father taught you such things?"

Clivo swallowed. "He said every kid needs structured activities. Helps keep us out of trouble."

"Structured activities? Bowling is structured; learning Hindustani is like being waterboarded." Douglas peered closely at Clivo. "Oh, yes, I see the wheels turning now. Things clicking into place, are they? So, why don't you mull that over for a bit. When you're ready to start work, give me a call. You have my card."

"The card was practically blank," Clivo said, his mind trying to process too many things at once.

"Just wave it in the air three times and I'll call you," Douglas said, opening the front door to another bolt of lightning and crack of thunder. Without another word he scurried to his big black car.

Clivo pulled the card out of his pocket and looked at it as Douglas's car retreated through the rain. He held on to it for a moment, a small part of him daring to believe that what Douglas had said was true, that his father had been carving a path for him. But after a quick moment, Clivo folded up the card and tossed it out the door and into the forest. He would believe that mythological creatures existed before believing his father had cared enough to do that.

Monday

"This math book will be your god for the next twelve weeks."

The thump of the large textbook on the metal desk startled Clivo. He lifted his cheek from his hand and tried to focus on the teacher in front of him. The guy was in his fifties and had an extremely bushy mustache and eyebrows and the nickname Professor Owl because he looked like a shaggy old coot.

"You are all here since, well, let's be honest, you are not the brightest bulbs of the bunch. But I am here to change all that! This may be called 'Remedial Math for Dummies'— oops, forget the 'for Dummies' part, that's just a joke between myself and the other teachers. Ahem, this may be called 'Remedial Math,' but I am here to turn your frowns upside down. My goal is to change you from kids who are one D-minus away from being the future burger flippers of America to being . . . crime fighters!"

Clivo looked around at the other fifteen students scattered throughout the sterile classroom. Some were paying close attention, but the majority had their heads down, either doodling on their notepads or checking their phones beneath their desks. It was the first day of school and already everyone was bored.

Clivo sat alone, as usual, in the corner. Even though he had gone to school with these kids since first grade, he didn't have many friends. He had been homeschooled by his mom, but after she died, his dad was gone too much to continue it. Aunt Pearl had gamely tried to homeschool him for a bit, but she didn't know much about history or geography or math or really anything except the Bible, her secret dancing, and how to properly brush a cat. So Clivo had joined the regular school partway through the year, where he quickly earned the title of "That Weird Mountain Kid." Before Pearl took over buying his clothes at Palace of Pants, his wardrobe had consisted of items his dad had brought back from his travels. Long cotton shirts from Turkey, harem pants from Bangladesh, a jade necklace from China. For the first year, all of the kids had pretended he was a foreign exchange student and spoken loudly and slowly in his face as if he didn't know English. Clivo's habit of accidentally blurting out words in other languages just made the kids laugh at him more.

A turning point had come during his first show-and-tell, when he brought some shrunken heads his dad had procured in Ecuador. Everyone freaked out (including his teacher, Mrs. Tuttle, who promptly threw up in a plant) except for Jerry, who asked to borrow one and hung it in his parents' shower to startle them. Jerry had pledged his allegiance as Clivo's best friend after that. Indeed, Jerry became the only kid allowed to play at Clivo's museum-like home (the other parents had turned their cars around the second they saw either the naked Polynesian statues out front or Russell practicing tai chi moves in a traditional outfit). Unfortunately, Jerry had ended up at a different middle school in sixth grade, leaving Clivo to once again sit alone at lunchtime.

"Remember, if you master math, you can—eventually—master accounting; if you master accounting, you can fight crime," Professor Owl continued, his breath blowing through his mustache. "The great gangsta Al Capone was finally sent to prison not because of his violent crimes—nay!—but because of the heinous atrocity of *tax evasion*. Even players get played."

Professor Owl laughed at his attempt at humor, but the class just stared at him with glassy eyes and slackened jaws. Not that the professor noticed as he joyously continued on with his spirited lesson.

Clivo stifled a yawn. He looked at Dan, the redheaded kid next to him, who was engrossed in a comic book that was strategically propped inside the math book. A fly was buzzing around Dan's head, so he dropped a hand from the book to shoo it away, allowing Clivo to see the comic's cover: *Chupacabra Man!* The inside showed brightly colored drawings of what looked to be an enormous humanoid lizard wearing a trucker hat and karate chopping some bad guys.

Clivo sniffed and turned his attention back to his textbook. But the damage was done. A picture of his father dueling with the chupacabra flashed through his mind. Clivo groaned and rubbed his eyes. Ever since Douglas had come to him the day before with the news about his father, Clivo had done everything in his power not to think about it. The part about his father chasing cryptids was just plain nuts, no two ways about it. But the part about his father training him for something was stuck in his head.

"To read a well-prepared tax return and unearth a hidden money-laundering scheme is nothing less than numerical poetry," Professor Owl hooted.

Clivo stared at the textbook, but his mind drifted again. Why *had* his father taught him so much stuff that, so far, didn't seem to have a purpose? Not many other kids could pick off a soda can at three hundred yards with a single-shot Winchester rifle. That wasn't something other parents did with their kids on the weekends, followed by a conversation in Russian at the local Cosmic Burger. Clivo had always thought the things his dad taught him were a little bizarre, but his *parents* had been bizarre.

A blur caught Clivo's eye and he saw Dan swatting furiously at the fly that was now bombarding his bowl-cut hair. Clivo tore a piece of notebook paper, rolled it up into a tight ball, and tossed it at the fly, knocking it out in mid-air.

"Thanks, Clivo," Dan said under his breath. "Just don't try to sit next to me again at lunchtime, okay? I don't hang out with kids whose clothes cost five bucks. You look homeless."

Clivo looked down at his blue-striped polyester sweater and oversized cargo pants, courtesy of Palace of Pants. "Okay. But just so you know, these clothes only cost *two* bucks." Clivo chuckled at his own lame joke.

Dan rolled his eyes and turned his head away. "Whatever."

Clivo sighed and went back to his thoughts.

After Douglas left, Clivo hadn't been able to resist doing some research. He had discovered that what the old man said was true. The Caparra Archaeological Site was indeed closed to private digs, and had been for years. But Clivo was sure that's where his dad had said he was going. Why would his father have lied to him about where he went on his work trip?

"Mr. Wren, perhaps you can recount how learning math can lead you to fighting crime? Unless the little bird on the tree out there has better advice on how you can earn your superhero cape?"

"Huh? Oh, sorry." Clivo swung his attention back to Professor Owl, who was staring at him with wide, challenging eyes. The rest of the class was staring at him, too, with a few kids snickering because he'd been caught spacing out. "I can fight crime by learning math because, um, Al Capone didn't know math very well so he ended up in prison. For tax invasion. I mean 'evasion.'"

Professor Owl's eyes went even wider before his face broke out into a huge grin. "Very good, Mr. Wren. *Very* good. You may want to consider a rewarding career as a tax auditor. Saving the world from gangsta tax cheats everywhere. Very noble indeed."

Clivo wished he shared Mr. Owl's enthusiasm, but becoming an auditor wasn't exactly the riveting future he had pictured for himself. Not that he had any clue what his future held—he certainly hadn't ended up in Remedial Math for Dummies because he was a good student. He'd never had any help with his studies at home. His dad had thought his time was better spent quizzing Clivo on survival skills, like which berries were edible and which were poisonous. Half the time, Clivo's homework was left forgotten in his backpack, especially because Aunt Pearl's face would glaze over in confusion whenever he asked her some kind of homework question.

But Clivo had never once gotten a scolding when he brought home his miserable report card. If his dad was home, he would just puff away on his pipe, look at the Cs and Ds, and let out a little snort. "Try to work hard enough to at least *stay in* school," was all he would say. But maybe his dad had been disinterested in his schoolwork because he'd already known that Clivo's destiny was to become a cryptid catcher.

Finally the bell rang, signifying the end of the school day. Clivo picked up his books and exited as quickly as possible. There was only one person who could help knock some sense into his head.

IV

After school, Clivo rode his bike to Taco Comet, a fast-food restaurant built in the shape of a silver saucer spacecraft, and picked up a paper sack of food that was incredibly unhealthy but totally delicious. He rode onward to the SETL Institute, where Jerry worked. The institute was a nonprofit organization dedicated to the Search for Extraterrestrial Life. Jerry had transferred from Clivo's school to the middle school across town because it had a better football program—a program that Jerry was quickly suspended from (as punishment for releasing a skunk into the school's ventilation system). Without football to keep him out of trouble, Mrs. Cooper had insisted she would get Jerry a babysitter to mind him after school, but Jerry had thrown a fit, saying that only babies had babysitters and, at thirteen, he should now be considered a man. So, Mr. Cooper, after talking to his boss about Jerry's rapscallion ways, created a low-level grunt job for Jerry at the institute. It seemed like a cool thing to Clivo, working at a place that searched for aliens, but Jerry said all he did was empty trash cans and fetch his dad coffee.

Clivo locked his bike to a scrawny tree outside the nondescript white building on the outskirts of town near the Air Force Academy. It looked like any old single-story office building, save for the myriad of antennas and satellites crammed on the roof. He walked into the polished white lobby and asked the receptionist if he could see Jerry.

Within a few moments, a loud click sounded and a heavy door opened to Clivo's right. Jerry stuck his head out, a large tin of Yummy Sniff instant coffee in his hand.

"Hey, Wren! How you doin'?"

Clivo smiled and held up the bag from Taco Comet. He knew from painful experience over his monthlong visit with the Coopers that Jerry's mom had the family eating like extremely healthy cavemen. "Just wanted to bring my buddy a snack. And I have a math problem I could use your help with."

Jerry stared at Clivo. The mention of a "math problem" was a code they had come up with while living together. It was an excuse for them to retreat to Jerry's room and play video games instead of watching old sitcom reruns with Mrs. Cooper after dinner. Now it just meant "I need to talk to you in private, immediately."

"Ah, sure, sure," Jerry said, glancing back over his

shoulder before opening the door wide. "Things are a little crazy in here right now, but every guy has to eat, right?"

Clivo stepped from the white lobby into the dark underbelly of the SETL Institute. The long, dimly lit hallway was glass on one side, revealing a large room whose other three walls were covered with projection screens that showed images of space and what looked to be sound waves. At least twenty people were staring intently at the screens in front of them, and it was obvious the whole room was crackling with excitement.

Mr. Cooper was standing in front of the biggest screen, his hand scratching his unshaven face. He waved at Clivo as he walked by, but then pointed at Jerry and made a sipping motion with his hands at his mouth, as if he needed more coffee, immediately.

"Something exciting going on?" Clivo asked.

"Umm, not really. You know how eager these guys are to find the first sign of intelligent life. It's probably just some space junk floating around."

Jerry opened the door at the end of the hall and they entered the fluorescent-lit break room.

"Please tell me you don't have anything healthy in that bag, because if I even look at another vegetable I will throw myself into traffic," Jerry pleaded, collapsing into a plastic chair. "Last night my ma announced she won't even allow milk at home anymore. Just almond milk. Almond! Like from a nut. I told her, if my milk doesn't moo, I'm not drinking it."

"Don't worry, I gotcha covered." Clivo opened the bag and shook out two overstuffed Taco Comet Supremo Burritos.

"Sweet, sweet bouncing baby! Wrenmaster, you are very close to making a grown man cry." Jerry gave his burrito a big kiss before ferociously chomping into it.

Clivo felt bad for his starving friend, so he handed over his burrito as well.

"So, I don't have much time, Pops needs his coffee," Jerry said between wolf bites. "What's your math problem?"

Clivo quickly gave him a rundown of his conversation with Douglas.

"He claimed your dad was a unicorn hunter?" Jerry asked, barely glancing up from his food.

"Basically, but apparently they haven't found a unicorn yet," Clivo said, cringing at how bizarre it sounded. "It sounds stupid, I know, but there are just some things that aren't adding up."

"Like what?" Jerry asked, distractedly glancing through the glass door to see what was going on in the main room.

"Like . . . why would my dad teach me five languages, jujitsu, and marksmanship?"

Jerry shrugged. "My dad taught me golf. Doesn't mean he wanted me to be Tiger Woods."

"Come on, Coops. You've always thought it was weird I could do all these things. Don't you think it's possible?"

Jerry wiped his mouth with a paper napkin from the bag. "No! I don't! Wren, listen to yourself. Killed by a *chupacabra*? It's ridiculous! When did you buy a ticket to the carnival and not exit at closing time?"

Clivo took a deep breath. Part of him was relieved his friend was saying this, but another part was disappointed. He hadn't realized how much he had begun hoping the whole crazy tale was true. "I know, I agree. It just got into my head that, you know, maybe my dad . . ." Clivo trailed off.

"I know, man," Jerry said, starting in on the second burrito. "I know you wish your relationship with your pops had been more solid. I feel you. But believing he had you in some kind of lassoer-of-legendary-animals boot camp is a bit cray cray, dontcha think?"

"Coops, you're following your dad into a job looking for aliens! Why is it so weird that I would follow my dad into a job looking for Bigfoot?" Clivo retorted.

Jerry exhaled heavily. He bundled together the empty wrappers and tossed them across the room toward a wastebasket. They bounced off the rim and landed near Clivo's feet. Clivo distractedly picked them up and threw them over his shoulder without looking. They landed perfectly in the basket.

Jerry eyed him and shook his head. "You're right. I'm

sorry. I shouldn't be such a harsh judge. What can I say? It's possible. Anything is possible, right?"

Clivo leaned forward again, his excitement gaining steam. "So, I did some research—"

"Of course you did," Jerry sighed, once again looking out the glass door.

"And aliens are considered cryptids. So, if they've found proof of aliens, then maybe, just maybe, other cryptids exist, too."

Jerry swung his eyes from the glass door and stared at Clivo in disbelief. "Are you asking me to tell you if my dad's found proof of extraterrestrial life?"

"I mean, I don't need details and all . . ."

"Clivo, I'm thirteen—as if my dad would tell me that stuff. Not even the president of the United States knows everything my dad knows."

"How is that possible?"

"SETL is a nongovernmental organization. The government quit giving us money back in 1993, so we're not required to tell them squat—no pay, no play. We could have three little green guys playing a mean game of poker downstairs and no one would know."

Clivo leaned forward, awestruck. "Do you?"

Jerry shot him a "really?" expression.

Clivo held his hands up. "Still, you could have found *something*. I'm not asking for details, Coops! Just maybe a subtle hint, a nod or something. I don't know, blink your

51

left eye once if you've found anything, just so I know what's possible."

"Blink my eye once? When did we leave planet Earth and fly to Loony Town?" Jerry exclaimed, a half-chewed bean flying out of his mouth. "Clivo, relax. We haven't found anything. And we won't. There's no such thing as extraterrestrial life."

Clivo sat back in his chair, once again disappointed. He barely registered the loud bells and whistles that were suddenly sounding from the main room.

"Are you sure?"

Jerry glanced again at the glass door, craning his neck to see what was going on. "Yes, I'm sure. And what do you mean 'aliens are considered cryptids'? Where do you get this stuff?"

"I looked it up on the internet," Clivo said. "Aliens are cryptids. They're in the same category as demons, angels, and fairies. Those are the myth-based ones. Then there's the other kind of cryptids that are more legend based, like Bigfoot, the Loch Ness Monster—" Clivo was speaking as quickly as possible so Jerry couldn't cut him off, but Jerry of course did.

"Whoa! So if we're talking about fairies and demons now, do you think Tinker Bell exists? Should I wear some garlic around my neck in case Dracula makes a house call?"

"Well, no . . ."

"Fine, they're myths and legends! That means 'stories,' Wren. Fake stuff. Created when people told them over a bonfire while dancing naked and roasting a saber-toothed tiger."

Clivo shook his head. "But listen, a lot of cryptids aren't just myths—they exist, because people have *seen* them. They're not just stories, they're scientific mysteries."

"There's no mystery with aliens. SETL has had cameras, satellites, microphones, robots, and sound waves scanning the universe since the 1980s. And nothing. I'm sorry, Wren, your dad was just a boring, absent archaeologist. And you're just a kid with mad language skills who keeps flunking out of English class for reasons I still don't understand. There's no magic unicorn that will change any of that."

Clivo nodded, his excitement deflating. He supposed he really had been hoping there was something magical out there that would make his life different than it was.

A loud gong sounded from the other room. Jerry quickly stood up.

"So, I should go, Dad probably needs his caffeine boost . . ."

The door to the break room crashed open and Mr. Cooper came running in. His eyeglasses were askew and his shirt was partially untucked. He looked like he had seen a ghost. Or an alien.

"Okay, Clivo, time to make like a rat and scurry away! Very important things are afoot." He quickly grabbed the tin of Yummy Sniff instant coffee and shoveled a spoonful of the dry crystals into his mouth. "Jerry, will you walk him out? Good to see you, Clivo! Maybe you can come for dinner on, say, Friday? Oooo, do I smell Taco Comet?"

Mr. Cooper ushered the two boys out of the break room into the hallway, and Clivo entered a hubbub of action. The main room of the SETL Institute was in chaos. Everyone was scrambling around, looking at screens or listening on headsets. A woman talking exuberantly on the phone noticed Clivo staring with his mouth agape, so she pulled a shade on one large pane of the glass wall, hiding the room from view.

"What was that all about?" Clivo asked Jerry once they were back in the lobby.

Jerry glanced at the receptionist, then motioned for Clivo to join him outside, where he began pacing and mumbling.

"You okay, Coops?" Clivo asked.

But Jerry kept pacing and mumbling, like he was engaged in a very serious discussion with himself.

"Coops?" Clivo asked again, wondering what was wrong with his friend.

Jerry quit his pacing and looked at Clivo as if Clivo had just kicked his dog or something. "Fine. UFOs exist! Are you happy?"

Clivo shook his head. "Wait, what?"

"They exist, okay? My dad has found three in his career. Maybe four. But ask me no further questions!"

Clivo was stunned. "Why haven't you ever told me this?"

Jerry paced faster and began kicking pebbles out of his way. "What was I supposed to do? Reveal one of the world's biggest secrets? This is top secret stuff, Wren. Like throw-you-in-a-concrete-cell-and-torture-you-for-information kinda stuff. My dad swore me to total secrecy on pain of death."

Clivo's head was swirling with so many questions he didn't know where to begin. "When did you find out about this?"

Jerry pursed his lips but finally blurted out, "My dad told me when I was a kid."

"Your dad *told* you?!"

"Well, he explained it to me after I broke into his desk at home and found photos."

Clivo looked down at the black asphalt of the parking lot, trying to make sense of this new world where aliens existed. "Do they look like green, wrinkled, bald men with big ears?"

Under the circumstances it was the only thing he could think of to say.

Jerry nodded. "Actually they do. Wait! I shouldn't have said that! Ask me no further questions! Just . . . I don't know what's going on with your all-of-a-sudden-incredibly-interesting family but . . . 'there are more things in heaven and earth than are dreamt of in your philosophy.' That's all I'm going to say."

"You just told me aliens exist and now you're quoting *Shakespeare*? Who are you and what have you done with my meathead friend?" Clivo asked, amazed.

At that moment the secretary, a short, grandmotherly woman with thick spectacles dangling from a chain of pearls, stuck her head out the door. "Jerry, darling, your father needs you. Time to say goodbye to your friend."

"Thank you, Mrs. Tarkenton, I'll be right there." The door closed and Jerry turned toward Clivo, a look of dead seriousness on his face. "Look, I honestly don't know if earthbound cryptids are real. I really don't. Maybe it's possible your dad was training you to become a—"

"Cryptid catcher," Clivo said, sticking his chin out proudly.

"Okay. Just . . . whether he was or not, be careful. If there's dangerous stuff out there, I can see you running straight toward it, just to prove something to your dad. Which is dumb because he's crossed over—sorry to be harsh. You may know some karate—"

"Jujitsu."

"Okay! But staying with Aunt Pearl whenever your dad was away over all these years hasn't exactly made you a tough guy. No offense, but you're kinda a wet noodle." Jerry ran to the door and yanked it open. "Just promise me you won't do anything crazy!"

Clivo threw his hands up in the air. "This, coming

from a guy running off to chase space invaders! And I'm not a wet noodle!"

Jerry slammed the door and motioned for Clivo to be quiet. He spoke in a hushed whisper. "They're harmless! With an insatiable appetite for ambercup squash. And yes you are!"

Jerry went back into the building, leaving Clivo standing in the beating sun, wondering what new world he had just entered.

V

Clivo rode his bike faster than he'd ever ridden it up
the dirt road to his house. The sun was beginning to drop
below the surrounding mountains, casting long shadows
from the tall, thin pine trees. The thick forest seemed to
close in around him and he jumped every time a squirrel
scurried through the crinkly dead leaves, his senses now on
high alert for whatever other creatures might be hiding in
the woods. Normally he enjoyed the shade provided by the
needled branches as he huffed and puffed his way up the
hill, but now the pockets of darkness from which numerous eyes could be watching gave him the chills. So he continued pedaling hard, eager to search his house for any
clues to the mystery he was facing.

He dropped his bike in the front yard and plowed
through the front door, tapping the coat of armor in his
usual ritual. "Hey, Bernie," he said distractedly.

After locking the cats in the kitchen, he ran into his
dad's study and began scanning it for some kind of sign that
Russell had been something other than the archaeologist

he had claimed to be. Clivo's eyes flicked around the room, looking for something, anything, that could be considered a hiding place. If his dad really was a cryptid catcher, he must have left *some* evidence behind.

He started with the dusty bookshelves, which were tightly packed with books. He pulled the tomes off one by one and flipped through them to see if there was anything hidden inside. But they were all what their covers advertised them to be—books on ancient civilizations and dinosaurs and a wide variety of other subjects, with nothing hidden amid the pages. Oddly, none of the books showed signs of heavy use, save for *Les Propheties*, the prophecy book by Nostradamus.

Next Clivo moved to the large mahogany desk. He riffled through the drawers, which were filled with *National Geographic* magazines and papers on *Australopithecus afarensis*. But everything was too fresh and too neat. The pages of the *National Geographic*s were stuck together as if they had never been flipped through. Why would his dad have so many books and magazines that he had never read? It was almost like Russell had set up a fake study to make him look like an archaeologist when he really wasn't. Encouraged, Clivo pulled the heavy drawers out completely and began looking for secret compartments. The thought that his dad had been training him for something—something greater than struggling through remedial classes—kept driving him. More importantly, if he found something, it meant that his dad had paid more attention to him than he had ever realized, that he hadn't been simply invisible to his father. Clivo pulled the drawers out faster.

But the desk revealed nothing, just empty holes where the drawers had been, with blank space behind them. Clivo stood with his hands on his hips, scanning the rest of the room. His eyes fell on the faded globe and his heart raced as he realized what a perfect hiding spot it was. He ran into the kitchen, grabbed a screwdriver, and tore the thing apart. He separated the two halves, but nothing was inside. No map, no coded instructions, no Zip drive to be plugged into a computer.

Clivo whirled around, desperate now. He tried to move the bookcases to see if there was a secret stairwell behind them, but they wouldn't budge. He moved his father's massive desk and rolled up the red carpet beneath it to see if there was a trapdoor that led to a hidden basement. Nothing.

He slumped into a chair. He was about to tear into the upholstery and pull the stuffing out, but he decided against it. Explaining to Pearl that he was destroying furniture because he thought his dad might have been a catcher of mythological beasts probably wouldn't go over so well.

Clivo looked around the room in disappointment and put the desk back in place before Aunt Pearl returned from her job washing dogs at the Humane Society.

Had his father ever said anything that was meant to be a clue? Russell must have planted some trail to the truth in case something happened to him. Catching beasts was probably pretty dangerous, and Russell must have known that. He wouldn't have risked something happening to him without leaving some kind of evidence behind as to what he did, right?

Clivo stood in the study and let the comforting smell of his dad's old meerschaum pipe wash over him. He was ready to give up the whole search and resign himself to a future of remedial classes when memories began flooding his head. He thought of the camping trips when his dad had taught him how to build a snow cave, of the conversations they had had in other languages, of the first time he had pinned his dad in a jujitsu practice. He remembered his dad's favorite saying: *"Some things are meant to be hidden. It's much better for the world to have its myths and its magic."* These were all signs that something was different about his life, but he needed more.

He left the study and looked at the artifacts from other countries that filled the house. Clay tablets from the Persian Empire leaned against one corner, a miniature stone obelisk from Ethiopia sat on a side table, and a jade necklace from the Shang Dynasty hung on a hook. Did any of these contain secret messages?

Clivo squatted by one of the clay tablets, running his fingers over the engraved cuneiform characters that looked like a bunch of slashes and triangles. His dad had taught him a lot of languages, but not that one.

With a sigh Clivo stood up, his eyes falling on Bernie, the suit of armor, and instantly his dad's voice filled his head.

"Bernie's a quiet fellow, but if he could talk, I'm sure he'd have a lot of secrets to tell. Don't you think so, C?"

The sound of the armor ringing as his dad rapped it with his knuckles echoed through Clivo's memory.

Mesmerized, Clivo approached Bernie, staring at the suit of armor as if it held the world's greatest treasure. His dad had brought the artifact back from a trip to England years before, and it was one of Clivo's favorite mementos. Bernie was taller and broader than Clivo, and his polished silver armor was dented in numerous spots. Clivo had spent hours picturing the battles Bernie must have been in, fighting his way fiercely through a throng of enemies with a broadsword. His dad had warned him not to touch it, but now his dad wasn't around.

Clivo reached up and lifted the visor on Bernie's helmet, the armor moving surprisingly easily on its hinges. He gasped as he saw a brass skeleton key dangling from a string with a note attached. With trembling hands he untied the string and unfolded the note, immediately recognizing his dad's handwriting:

ONE COUNTRY, ABOVE ALL, HOLDS THE KEY TO MY HEART. ONE TURN IS ALL YOU GET; FIND THE DIFFERENCE.

Clivo's stomach flipped with excitement, then dropped in confusion. What was that supposed to mean? It was obviously a clue about what the key opened, but Clivo had no idea what it meant. What country had held the key to his father's heart?

He glanced around the room, noticing several locked chests and cupboards. He could simply try the key on all of them, but according to the note he only got one turn. One turn at what?

Clivo forced himself to calm down and think. What country had held the key to his father's heart? Clivo went over all their conversations, trying to remember if his dad had talked more about one country than another.

He began wandering aimlessly around the house, lost in thought. At one point he glanced up and noticed a photo of his mom on the wall. She was standing on a ski slope, her joyful face smiling as she held her arms out wide to the snow-covered peaks stretching behind her, her blond curls peeking out from under her woolen hat.

Bingo.

His mom had been born in Brunei to hippie parents who'd thought that being born in a rain forest would bless their daughter with special powers. Clivo wasn't sure about that, but she had definitely held a special power over his dad, because Russell had adored her. Brunei must have been the country that held the key to his father's heart, because that's where Clivo's mom was from.

Clivo whirled around the room, trying to remember the artifact his dad had brought back from his trip to Brunei. But nothing rang a bell.

Then he remembered the attic.

He raced up the steps covered in a worn carpet from Turkey and pulled a rope that opened a ceiling hatch. A rickety ladder slid down and he eagerly scrambled up it.

The attic was dark and dusty and stuffed with souvenirs and trinkets that didn't fit in the rest of the house. It was like the closet in a museum, a place where forgotten treasures languished in the dark. Clivo lifted the plastic sheets draped over various sculptures and pottery, but there was nothing that required a key to be opened.

He walked along the floor, which creaked with each step, beginning to wonder if he was totally on the wrong path. Then he saw what he was looking for, and everything made perfect sense.

Clivo hurried to a far corner and knelt by a large chest, which his father had brought back from Brunei. It was made of sturdy wood and covered in studded brown leather. He examined the trunk and furrowed his brow in disappointment. Instead of one lock to open the top, the trunk was covered with at least a dozen locks that opened various drawers and compartments of all different sizes.

Wedged under the chest was a weathered piece of parchment that Clivo delicately pulled out, the elegant script barely visible in the late-afternoon light filtering through the small attic window.

The Chest of Dreams

Hide your items of importance here. But be warned. The key opens one lock, and one lock alone. If the wrong choice is made, liquid vials will mix and dissolve the contents in a puff of smoke. The smoke is harmless when breathed in, but it will send you into a deep sleep, where dreams of your evil plundering will haunt you for ages to come. Choose wisely.

Clivo shuddered, both at the idea of losing whatever contents were inside and at the idea of being haunted in his dreams.

He held the key up to all the different locks, wondering which one it fit into, but all the keyholes appeared to be the same size. He scrubbed his fingers through his hair in frustration. How was he supposed to know which lock was the right one?

"One turn is all you get; find the difference."

Clivo again ran his hands over the tough leather, his fingers tracing the decorated brass locks tarnished with age. Then he spied something else. Engraved on each lock was a symbol, barely visible in the low light.

He rummaged in a box next to him that his dad had used to store their camping gear and pulled out a candle.

He lit the wick with a waterproof match and held the flickering glow to the symbols. They all appeared to depict animals, probably from Brunei, including a tiger, an elephant, and a rhinoceros.

There didn't seem to be anything remarkable about the engravings until Clivo noticed one on a narrow compartment that stood out from the rest. This creature he didn't recognize. It had the small body of a frog and the large head of a crocodile, complete with a long snout and pointed teeth.

This couldn't have been a real animal. Not that Clivo knew every animal on Earth, but he was pretty sure he would've heard about one that was half frog, half crocodile.

Compared to the other engravings, this one definitely was different. To boot, it might even be a cryptid, which furthered Clivo's conviction that this was the right drawer to unlock.

He took a deep inhale and inserted the key into the lock. He held his breath and pointed his face away as the key turned, in case a plume of smoke came out and sent him into haunted dreams.

Instead, the lock clicked harmlessly and the drawer slid open.

Clivo paused for a nervous moment before reaching inside and pulling out a brown leather-bound photo album. An old one, by the looks of it. The cover was cracked and faded, the leather dotted with water spots.

Clivo's heart dropped in disappointment. He wasn't sure what he had been expecting, but he had hoped that the mysterious contents inside would be much more exciting than an old album.

But then he saw the pages and gasped in surprise.

The first photo, a Polaroid, showed a picture of his dad from years before, judging by his short shorts and luxuriant mustache. He was kneeling on the ground, a tranquilizer gun in his hand, and by his feet was a large, scaly creature with a scorpion's tail and saber teeth. Cursive writing in the corner of the photo read *Dingonek, 1987, Namibia*.

Clivo flipped the pages in silence. Some of the photos were older than others, and his dad's hair and clothes varied in style. Russell was smiling in each one, and there was always an unconscious creature at his feet. The writing on each photo described the creature—*Buru*; *Beast of Bray Road*; *Tatzelwurm*—as well as the date and location where it had been caught.

Another picture showed Russell with his arm around a tall, hairy, unconscious creature propped up with its tongue lolling out. The stem of Russell's pipe was between his smiling lips as one hand gave a peace sign. The corner of the photo read *Honey Island Swamp Monster, 2014, Louisiana*.

Clivo flipped another page and his breath caught. His father was not alone in this picture. He was holding a wombat-like creature with antlers, and next to him was

Clivo's mom, smiling widely and wearing a handkerchief on her head. In her arms was a baby who was happily patting the back of what was labeled a *gunni*.

A real family photo. And they all seemed so happy together, the way Jerry's family looked in all of their photos. One of Clivo's small, chubby hands reached up for Russell, who was looking down at him with a secretive, knowing smile. Clivo ran his finger over the photo, trying to memorize the scene. He barely had any memories of them all together, and seeing them as a loving family unit made his chest swell with happiness. For a moment he forgot all about the unconcious gunni slung on his father's arm.

Clivo turned another page and a sheet of paper fell out. He unfolded it and realized it was a copy of the contract Douglas had shown him, his baby footprint stamped at the bottom. Clivo hadn't realized his mouth had opened in disbelief, and he had to quickly slurp up some spit before it fell on the document.

He might not have been knocked out by sleep-inducing smoke, but he sure felt like he was about to faint from shock.

VI

Clivo sat in the attic for a long time. He didn't feel the stifling air pressing on him, didn't notice the dust motes that swirled around his face. His mind was a million miles away.

His dad had been a cryptid catcher. Clivo was certain of it now. But his initial rush of excitement was turning into confusion. Why hadn't his dad ever told him any of this? Why had his dad spent so many years keeping this a secret when he could have just told Clivo the truth? Life as Clivo had known it had been a lie, when the truth would have been so much easier.

Clivo pushed aside his questions and looked at the contract that was still clutched in his hand, at his inked baby footprint faded from the years. He knew he was terrible at school, but maybe, just maybe, he'd make a decent cryptid catcher.

Without another thought, he grabbed his wallet, where he thought he had stashed Douglas Chancery's calling card. But the card wasn't there. Clivo frantically looked in every pocket and groaned as he remembered throwing it into the forest.

He climbed down from the attic, setting the album carefully on the dining room table. He ran out of the house and into the dark woods, scrambling on his hands and knees through the wet leaves. A frightened skunk ran off, its tail lifted high in the air.

After a few minutes of searching he finally saw something silver peeking out from a pile of pine needles and grabbed it.

Clivo ran inside, slamming the door on the swarm of mosquitoes that had almost sucked him dry. He carefully laid the card on the dining room table, uncrinkling the thin, foil-like material.

But immediately he furrowed his brow. He'd forgotten that there wasn't anything on the card. Nothing but the man's name.

Clivo kicked the table in frustration and promptly began hopping around in pain from a stubbed toe. Douglas was gone, and Clivo had no way of contacting him.

Or did he? What was it that Douglas had said about getting in touch with him? Just wave the card in the air three times, wasn't it?

Clivo picked up the card and self-consciously looked around, wondering if it had been some kind of a joke. Feeling silly, he waved it exuberantly three times over his head. The card lit up with a soft glow, as if something had been activated.

Instantly his phone buzzed. The screen read *Unknown Number.*

"Hello?" Clivo asked tentatively, bringing the phone to his ear.

"Hello?" a gruff voice asked at the other end.

"Uh, Mr. Chancery?"

"Who's this?"

"It's Clivo Wren, sir."

"Who?"

Clivo rubbed his eyes. "You called me! Clivo Wren, Russell Wren's son."

"Oh, the brat. Well, what do you want?"

"Well, sir, I'm . . . um . . . I'm ready to become a cryptid catcher."

"Took you long enough. I'll be right over."

Thirty minutes later, there was a knock at the door. Clivo opened it to find Douglas on the porch.

"Clivo Wren?" Douglas asked in his gravelly voice. A rumble of thunder sounded in the distance, as if on cue.

"Yes?"

"Do you know who I am?"

"We've been through this before, Mr. Chancery. Please just come in."

"Oh, right. You're the kid with no appreciation for the dramatic." He hobbled inside and handed Clivo his jacket.

71

Clivo led Douglas into the study and gave him the photo album.

"So, I found this." Clivo eyed Douglas carefully, half worried that the old man would burst out laughing and reveal that this was all a silly prank and Clivo should go back to his math homework.

Instead, Douglas took his time flipping through the pages, his voice crackling with nostalgia. "Look at that dingonek, she was a real beauty. Although your dad's taste in shorts had something to be desired. Ah! The gunni! She was a tricky one; your dad and mom traveled halfway across Australia to find her. And look at that dopey smile on your face."

Clivo protectively took the album from Douglas.

"So this is all true, then?"

"Is what all true?" Douglas asked.

"That the immortal cryptid exists and I'm supposed to find it?" Clivo threw his arms up in exasperation, a gesture he made frequently whenever Douglas was around.

"Yes, of course! I told you that the first time I was here, you dummy."

Clivo ignored the insult and tried to sift through all the questions he had. "And was my mom one, too?"

Douglas heaved his body into a chair with a long grunt. "Nah. She followed your dad on some of his quests, though, because he hated being away from you when you were a baby. Why, I have no idea. All drool and slobber, to me.

But once you got older I put a stop to that. All the world needs is some snot-nosed little kid letting everyone know that mythological creatures exist. So she focused on training you, until the grim reaper visited her, if you know what I mean."

Lightning flashed through the window, thunder boomed, and a sudden gust of rain pattered on the panes of glass. The heater kicked on, a deep rattling from the basement sounding through the brass vents. Clivo took the chair next to Douglas.

"Was my mom . . . you know?"

Douglas wrinkled his nose. "Was she what?"

Clivo took a deep breath. He wasn't sure he wanted the answer to the next question. "Was she . . . killed . . . by a cryptid, too?"

"Oh. No. The cancer got her. I thought you knew that."

"I did know that, it's just—"

"Then why are you asking me questions you know the answers to? Are you a dimwit?"

"No. I mean, I'm in some remedial classes, but I don't think—"

"Remedial classes? Don't you speak five languages?"

"Yeah, but I don't get school credit for them."

"Fabulous, an official dummy." Douglas pulled a cigar from the inside of his jacket and clamped his teeth around it. "Mind if I smoke?"

"Well . . ."

"Thanks." He lit the cigar and began blowing smoke rings. The old man sat comfortably back in his chair and stared. Clivo stared back, waiting for Douglas to begin speaking, but Douglas just sat there, puffing on his cigar. Clivo shifted uncomfortably. The old man's gaze was penetrating, like he was studying Clivo or taking his measure. He probably wondered if Clivo had what it took to be a catcher. Clivo was wondering the same thing himself.

"Sooooo," Clivo began.

"So, any questions before you go on your first quest?"

"About a hundred—"

"You find a cryptid, you tranquilize it, you check its blood. If it's not the immortal cryptid you let it go. If it is, you sit with it and keep it company until I get there. Got it? Good, I think we're done here."

Douglas made as if to stand up.

"Whoa! I said I have a few questions!" Clivo said, panicked that Douglas would run off without leaving him with some idea about how to go about becoming a catcher.

"I just explained everything to you! It's only four steps! Even a remedial kid should be able to follow four steps!"

Clivo sighed and rubbed his hands over his face. "Can you just go through everything slowly with me, please?"

"Such as?"

"Such as how do I find creatures that aren't supposed to exist?"

"Simple. Do what your father did . . . Get me a scotch, would you? It smells like a hippie tent in here and it's bothering my throat."

Clivo dragged himself from his chair to the kitchen and poured Douglas a ginger ale.

"Any chance you'd help me out and tell me how my father did it?" Clivo asked when he returned to the study and handed Douglas the drink while waving the acrid cigar smoke away from his face.

"Find a reliable group of conspiracy theorists," Douglas said, taking out his flask and adding more liquid to his drink. "Those whack jobs spend more time researching the mysteries of the world than bona fide scientists do. And they're not bound by a sense of reason, so the stuff they come up with is usually spot-on. Just don't tell them that cryptids *actually* exist or you'll spoil all their fun. And for gawd's sake, especially don't mention the immortal cryptid. The last thing we need is for some crazy nerd to find it. He'll build his own immortal world populated with fellow crazies who have no reflexes. Our professional sports programs would go down the tubes. It would be a disaster."

Clivo was having a hard time keeping up with everything Douglas was throwing at him. "And what do I tranquilize them with?"

"Tranquilizer darts."

"That I get from . . ." Clivo left the sentence hanging, hoping Douglas would fill in the rest.

"Oh, right. I've got the darts and the blood sampler in my car. Don't let me forget to give them to you. Ha! That would make your quest a bit more difficult, wouldn't it?"

Douglas laughed heartily until he fell into a coughing fit. Clivo gently patted the old man on the back as he wheezed. "Oh, and here's a list of all the possible cryptids with the ones your dad found crossed out." He pulled a leather-bound notebook from a back pocket and handed it to Clivo.

Clivo untied the string closing the notebook and read the pieces of parchment inside. There were at least a thousand names on the list.

"That's a lot of cryptids to find," Clivo said, amazed that so many of the creatures might exist in the world.

"You ain't kidding," Douglas replied.

Clivo read some of the names, most of which he didn't know, like the adjule and the Beast of Exmoor. That one sounded ominous.

"Are these all earthbound cryptids?" Clivo asked.

Douglas sputtered, "Of course they're earthbound! What do you think I'm going to do? Launch you into space? Now let's wrap this up, I'm getting peckish."

Clivo had so many more questions, he didn't know where to begin, and he wanted to ask one that wouldn't get him yelled at. "Does the government know about the immortal cryptid?"

"Bah! The *government*. Maybe. Maybe not. Doesn't

really matter, as they're not putting any resources into finding it. Ask them to fund the building of a bomb, no problem. Ask them to fund the search for an animal that cures death, forget it. Fascists! Nope, you're on your own with this one, kid."

"But you said my dad was making sure the immortal cryptid didn't fall into the wrong hands. So, there must be other people searching for it?" Clivo asked.

Douglas stubbed out his cigar and blew a final plume of smoke.

"There are plenty of other people looking for it. Mostly privately funded. Some petulant kid pop star with bleached hair has two guys on his payroll. Hopefully *that* guy doesn't become immortal; we'd all be forced to wear skinny jeans forever. There are a couple of catchers from Luxembourg, but they're idiots. Good thing, too. All we need is an immortal world of Luxembourgers speaking Luxembourgish. I'd launch *myself* into space. And then you've got your standard lot of criminals and mercenaries who work for the highest bidder. Speaking of which, here you go."

Douglas fished in his wallet and pulled out a credit card.

"What's this?" Clivo asked.

"That's a Diamond Card to buy anything you need. But keep your receipts, I want to make sure you're not blowing my money on nonessential things like food."

Clivo looked at the card in wonder. It wasn't plastic,

like most credit cards, but metal, with a little diamond chip embedded in it. It hadn't even occurred to him how he would actually pay for these quests. Or get out of school to do so. He figured Pearl wouldn't be too willing to write a note saying he was excused from classes on account of going legendary-creature catching. Speaking of which . . .

"Does Aunt Pearl know about all this?" Clivo asked, his eyes going wide at the thought of his aunt chasing after Bigfoot, her salsa-dancing skirt flowing behind her.

"Shoot, no. And best to keep it that way. She's not the sharpest tool in the shed, if you know what I mean." Douglas fished in his other pocket and pulled out a large smartphone, a kind that Clivo had never seen before. It looked heavy and waterproof. "That's an ultra-secure satellite phone that only connects to me. You can send me texts, pictures, video, anything. Try not to bother me with every little question about life, though. Hand me your regular phone," he said, passing the smartphone to Clivo.

"Huh?" Clivo asked, instantly engrossed in looking at his new phone.

"Come on, let me see it," Douglas said, making a "give me" motion with his hand.

Clivo pulled the phone out of his pocket and handed it to Douglas, who quickly placed it on the floor and crushed it with his cane.

"Hey!" Clivo said. "That was my phone!"

"It's also a darned good tracking device if the other catchers want to follow you. Everyone knows your father was the best, and they'll expect you to be the same. It also guarantees you can't use social media while you're in the field. All I need is a selfie of you splashed across the internet next to the Ayia Napa Sea Monster."

Next Douglas handed him a wad of cash and Clivo's face froze. It was more money than he had ever seen in his entire life.

"There's ten grand in petty cash," Douglas continued. "But again, receipts. Your clothes are atrocious and I don't need you buying a whole new dapper wardrobe with my funds." Douglas stood up with a grunt. "Now, this arduous conversation killed my soul about ten minutes ago, so I'm going to make my exit."

"Okay," Clivo said, feeling extremely overwhelmed by everything. He retrieved the old man's jacket and opened the front door. The thunder had passed, but the rain continued to fall.

Douglas went to his car and returned with a silver metal case. The wind had picked up, leaving bits of leaves in his wild hair.

"Here are your tranquilizers, tranquilizer gun, and blood sampler, user guides included." Douglas handed over the case.

"Just one more question," Clivo quickly interjected before Douglas could leave.

"Oh, for heaven's sake, WHAT?"

Clivo looked down at the wooden floor. It was a question he hated asking, but Douglas was the only person alive who could answer it. "So my dad really thought I could do this? Be a good cryptid catcher?"

"No, he taught you five languages so you would know what to order in an ethnic restaurant. How should I know? He trained you; what difference does it make what he thought?" He gave Clivo a sturdy pat on the shoulder and retreated to his car. "Good luck, kid. Don't mess it up."

As Douglas drove off, Clivo stood in his doorway, feeling completely adrift, his arms filled with the Diamond Card, satellite phone, case, and money, and his head swimming with the realization that he had no idea where to find a conspiracy theorist group that could locate mythological creatures.

VII

Clivo shut the door and laid everything Douglas had given him on the round dining room table. From the shelves in his dad's study he retrieved *Les Propheties*, carefully placing it next to the photo album on the table. He wanted everything of importance in one place to help him sort through his thoughts, which were a jumbled mess.

He had opened his laptop and was staring at the screen when he heard Aunt Pearl's Pinto pull up in the driveway, thumping from the heavy drumbeat of her favorite music.

Clivo jumped to his feet. He had been so caught up in everything that he had forgotten about his guardian. He grabbed the stuff on the table and let the cats out of the kitchen. They instantly sprang all over him, desperately trying to smother him with pent-up love and affection.

With felines in pursuit, Clivo ran upstairs and found a safe spot for all the cryptid catcher supplies at the back of his closet. Just as he heard Pearl's footsteps climbing up the stairs, he lay down in bed and pulled the sheet over his head. He pretended to be asleep, snoring a little bit and trying to avoid yelping as the cats pawed his face through the cover.

The door squeaked open and Pearl looked in on him.

"Aw, isn't that the cutest thing?" she whispered. "Goodnight, sweet munchkins. Watch over my little rascal for me."

The door closed and Clivo flung the sheet off his head, scattering purring cats in every direction. He fetched his laptop and got to work with his web browser. In the search field on his home page, he typed *mythological creatures* and *conspiracy*. The search yielded *790,000* results. That was shocking. He'd figured there was a hearty interest in UFOs, but he hadn't realized so many people were invested in finding the Sasquatch. Out of curiosity, Clivo looked up other conspiracy groups and found that they existed for just about everything you could think of. Of course there were the usual ones: *Who really killed JFK? Was the moon landing real? Is Elvis still alive?* But then there were some wacky ones: *Is the moon itself even real? Are Nestlé Toll House cookies really made by elves?* And *Were the Founding Fathers actually zombies who now run a casino in North Dakota?* (That group had over twenty thousand members.)

Finally he stumbled across an active chat room on IMythsThePast.com that was discussing what breed of horse Pegasus was. Between heated exchanges about whether or not he was a "true white" horse or just an albino Clydesdale, Clivo joined the conversation under a screen name.

SaveMeFromtheCats: Hi, guys. Does anyone have an idea about where I can find a cryptid? Preferably somewhere close to Colorado. It's for a school project. Thank you.

He felt weird asking such a question and was glad these chat rooms were anonymous.

Monticore: Hey, dum dum, this is a mythozoology site, not a cryptozoology site. Get your creatures straight.
SaveMeFromtheCats: Oh, sorry. What's the difference?
Monticore: What's the difference? I'm done here. Isn't anyone monitoring this thing to filter out the riffraff?
I'mYourVenus: Calm down, Monticore. SaveMe, mythos are magical creatures, sometimes gods, that exist in a veil beyond our world.
Monticore: And cryptids are STUPID.
I'mYourVenus: I apologize for him. Cryptids are hidden animals that have, at some point, been seen

by humans but whose existence has never been verified by science.

Monticore: BECAUSE THEY'RE DUMB.

SaveMeFromtheCats: Oh, okay. Sorry, guys. I guess I'm in the wrong chat room. Have a good night.

I'mYourVenus: You too! You sound cute!

Monticore: Flee, worthless plebeian!

Clivo clicked out of the chat room as quickly as possible.

He spent the next four hours researching cryptozoology websites and dropping in on various other chat rooms. The amount of information was staggering. Those who were believers were really into this stuff, especially when it came to Bigfoot. There was the Finding Bigfoot Project, the Bigfoot Search Party, the Bigger Bigfoot Search Party, and more. Most of these groups were dedicated to finding scientific proof of Bigfoot's existence, or, better yet, Bigfoot himself, except for the Grab Your Gun Group, which sponsored military-style hunts with the goal of killing the creature. It seemed odd to Clivo that a group would want to kill something they obviously found fascinating.

Clivo wondered for a moment why his dad had never caught Bigfoot, since there was so much information on this creature; then he shook his head at how weird it was to ask himself that.

He researched a few other cryptids, like the shunka warak'in and the Ozark Howler, but all of the information he found was pretty general—a list of reported sightings, possible footprints, eerie mating calls heard at night. There wasn't anything specific about how to stalk one beyond recommendations on bait, camouflage clothing, and night-vision video cameras.

The downstairs clock chimed one A.M., and Clivo yawned and gave himself a stretch. He opened his bedroom window, hoping the cool air would wake him up. The rain had stopped, leaving behind the calming sound of water dripping off the gutters. He took a few deep breaths and realized he was going nowhere fast. If there were groups out there who really knew how to find a cryptid, he first had to find *them*.

He creaked open his bedroom door and listened. After a moment he heard what sounded like an angry, huffing cow. It was Pearl's loud snoring.

As quietly as possible, he pulled open the attic hatch, unfolded the rickety ladder, and climbed back up. In his haste to look at the photo album he had forgotten to see if there was anything else inside the chest.

He crossed the room and peered inside the open drawer. His heart sank when all he saw was emptiness.

But on closer inspection he noticed that tucked in the back, half wedged in the corner, was what looked to be a business card. He pulled it out, being careful not to tear it.

International Cryptozoology Museum
The World's Finest Cryptozoological Museum

Beneath this was an address in Portland, Maine, as well as a poorly drawn Bigfoot and the hours of operation (*Open seven nights a week*). He flipped the card over and instantly recognized his dad's handwriting on the back. There was just one word: *cyborg*.

Clivo let out a long exhale of relief. He wasn't sure what it meant, but it was something.

Now what? He supposed the next step was to call them and ask if they knew the exact locations of any cryptids. It was worth a shot; it was a museum, after all.

Clivo snuck back to his room (almost tripping on Ricky Martin, who was perched at the base of the ladder) and grabbed the secret satellite phone. He knew the museum was closed, but he just wanted to make sure the place still existed. The phone had rung once when an irritated voice picked up.

"You better be on fire."

"Excuse me?" Clivo asked. The voice sounded disturbingly familiar.

"I said you better be on fire because that's the only

86

reason you should be calling me at two in the morning, you nincompoop."

"Oh, sorry, Mr. Chancery. I wasn't trying to call you."

It sounded like mariachi music was playing loudly in the background.

"What do you mean, you weren't trying to call me? I told you this phone only connects to me. Obviously you need remedial classes for the remedial."

"Sorry, I just got a lead on something and was trying to research it. And since you broke my phone I didn't know what else to do." Clivo tried to keep his voice at a whisper, but he knew from experience that nothing short of a bullhorn in Aunt Pearl's ear would wake her up.

Douglas spit something from between his lips and sputtered, "You were trying to *call* a lead? Never do anything by phone! What are you, an amateur?"

Clivo dropped his head back and squeezed his eyes shut. "So how am I supposed to contact these people? And feel free to answer without yelling at me."

"I'll give you a hint. You get on, it flies you somewhere, you get off." Douglas yelled at someone across the room. "*Señor! Mas tequila, por favor! Gracias.* By the way, the Mexican food in this town stinks."

"Where do you live, anyway?" Clivo asked, wondering where Douglas was visiting from. Hopefully it was very far away.

"Where I reside is none of your business," Douglas said with a burp.

Clivo rolled his eyes. "Fine. Anyway, you're saying I should get on an airplane and *fly* to talk to these people?"

"Exactamundo." Douglas took a noisy drink of something and went into a raucous coughing fit. When he recovered, his voice was even raspier. "You've got the Diamond Card. Unless you've managed to lose it already."

"No, no, I still have it," Clivo said, quickly checking his wallet to make sure he hadn't dropped it. "But I have school tomorrow."

Douglas sighed heavily. "Kid, as we speak, some very dangerous people are searching for the immortal cryptid. Now, you can either go to school tomorrow and learn what kind of toilet paper George Washington used, or you can GET YOURSELF OUT THERE AND SAVE THE WORLD."

Clivo winced and held the phone away from his ear. "Okay, okay. I'll skip school."

"Good. Oh, I forgot to tell you something very, very important."

Clivo sat down, hoping Douglas was about to give him some extremely useful information. "Okay."

"Make sure you fly coach."

Tuesday

VIII

Clivo got back into bed after hanging up with Douglas and instantly fell asleep. Before he knew it the sun was streaming through his window and Aunt Pearl was tapping on his door.

"Clivo, honey, aren't you going to be late for school?"

"I'll be down in a minute, Aunt Pearl," Clivo said, bounding out of bed and grabbing his laptop.

Clivo had to come up with a way to sneak away from Aunt Pearl for a few days. He felt terrible lying to her, but he didn't have any other option. He could wait until winter break to search for a cryptid, but that was three months away and some bad guy could have found the immortal by then. Clivo figured there was only one way to get Aunt Pearl out of the house, so he woke his computer out of sleep mode and did an internet search, hoping he'd get lucky and find just the thing. After a few clicks, he found what he was looking for:

Regional Salsa Dancing Competition
Wednesday, August 23–Sunday, August 27

Ballroom, Holiday Inn off Highway 336
Cash prizes! Five days of festivities!
Sheridan, Wyoming

Using the internet phone call feature in his e-mail app, he called the Wyoming hotel and made his first use of his Diamond Card. They treated him as a prankster at first, but were happy to do whatever he requested once he mentioned the name of the credit card.

Then he called Aunt Pearl. He heard the loud bongo ringtone on her cell phone and the clank of a pan as she placed it in the sink.

"Hola!" Aunt Pearl's cheery voice said as she answered the phone.

Clivo did his best to deepen and disguise his voice. "Is this Aunt—I mean Miss Aunt Pearl Wren?"

"I have the pleasure of being me!" she happily replied.

Clivo cleared his throat. "Well, Miss Wren, word of your salsa skills has made it all the way up here to Wyoming. We know it's last minute, but we've had a sudden cancellation by one of our star participants and would love to invite you up for five days of fun at our regional dance competition."

Aunt Pearl gasped and Clivo heard the scrape of a chair being pulled out as she sat down. "You've heard of *me*?"

"We have, we hear you can cha-cha really well," Clivo continued.

"I can cha-cha like a champ!" Aunt Pearl said excitedly. "Except the cha-cha is not salsa dancing."

This was news to Clivo. "Of course! Anyway, we think you might have a chance at the first-place trophy in this year's competition."

Aunt Pearl gasped again. "A *trophy*? I've always dreamed of winning my own trophy!"

"Wonderful!" Clivo said, thrilled that his plan was working. "So, we'll see you up here today, as quickly as possible. We have already covered your hotel and registration fees. And feel free to bring your cats. The hotel is animal friendly," he added, having confirmed on the phone that this was true.

Aunt Pearl let out a moan. "I can't."

"Excuse me?" Clivo asked, his stomach dropping. "What could possibly be in the way of your dancing glory?"

Aunt Pearl spoke in a hushed whisper. "I'd love to come, but I have a *teenager* at home. And from everything I've read, they should not be left alone for too long or things get set on *fire* or are stolen, or general mischief happens! I read it in a book on raising teens."

Clivo ran his hands through his hair and cursed whoever had written that book (although he thought Jerry's parents could probably use a copy). "And how long has this teenager been a teenager?" he finally asked.

"Um, since June. I'm sorry, since August. His thirteenth birthday was in August."

"Then there's nothing to worry about, Miss Wren! It takes a while for teenagers to morph into hooligans. Your teenager should be well-behaved for at least a couple more years."

"But the book says . . ." Aunt Pearl replied, her voice sounding uncertain.

"I did mention the first-place cash prize, didn't I, and the promise of dancing glory?" Clivo asked insistently. "I assure you, your teenager will be just fine for a few days. If not, we will happily pay for anything that is burned down while you're away."

Aunt Pearl was quiet for a few moments, her breathing heavy against the receiver. "You promise my little rascal will be okay?"

Clivo once again felt a pang of guilt for lying. He wished he could just tell her the truth about the immortal, but Douglas had warned him not to. And his dad must have had a good reason for not telling her about cryptid catching, so it was probably best that he didn't, either. "Your little rascal will be just fine. Now, please hurry, Miss Wren, the competitions are beginning tomorrow."

"Okay," Aunt Pearl said with resolve, "but you better hold on to your shoes, because my Cuban-style cross step is going to blow your socks off!"

Clivo gave Aunt Pearl all the information he could find on the website, then threw on some clothes, brushed his teeth, and headed downstairs, doing his best to look innocent. He entered the kitchen, where the smell of pancakes mixed with the sound of cats wailing beside their empty food bowls.

Aunt Pearl looked up from the stove with a sheepish expression. "Hi, sleepyhead, here's some pancakes and fresh maple syrup." She slid him a plate of pancakes that had dabs of butter on them in the shapes of smiley faces.

"Thanks, Aunt Pearl." Clivo fed the cats, then took a seat on a barstool and stuffed some food in his mouth, doing his best not to look at her. He tried to remember that even though he had lied, a five-day getaway spent dancing was probably Aunt Pearl's idea of heaven.

Aunt Pearl slowly wiped the counter with a sponge, her face worried. "So, um, I just got a phone call this morning and I've been invited to a very special retreat this week in Wyoming. Would you be okay if I left you alone for a few days?"

Clivo let out a dramatic sigh. "I'll be okay, Aunt Pearl. I know how important church is to you. And you just bought plenty of mac and cheese, so I'll be fine."

Aunt Pearl pouted her lip. "And you promise not to set anything on fire?"

Clivo laughed. "Yes, Aunt Pearl, I promise not to set anything on fire."

"Or cause mischief?"

"No mischief," Clivo promised, unsure if getting on an airplane to search for legendary creatures was considered mischief.

Aunt Pearl relaxed her shoulders and pinched his cheeks. "You're my little rascal, you know that?" And with that, Aunt Pearl wrestled the cats into their travel carriers, then tore upstairs, threw some clothes into a suitcase, and ran back down within minutes, her salsa-dancing heels clicking on the wooden stairs as the cats meowed loudly. "Okay, sweetheart, I'll be back Monday. Be a good boy, and please don't steal any cars while I'm away."

"No guarantees, but I'll do my best," Clivo joked.

As soon as Aunt Pearl had peeled her Pinto out of the driveway, Clivo grabbed his satellite phone and made a call. He winced as a groggy voice picked up.

"You are literally killing me," Douglas mumbled at the other end.

"Sorry, Mr. Chancery, but can you call a taxi to take me to the airport?"

"You can order it yourself from the internet, you cretin."

Clivo spoke the next part as quickly as possible. "Well, could you at least call my school and disguise your voice as Aunt Pearl and tell them I'll be out sick for the rest of the week?"

Douglas agreed, but muttered something so filthy that

if Aunt Pearl heard it she would have stuck a bar of soap in his mouth.

Clivo arrived at the Denver airport forty minutes later and handed the driver the fare and a tip from his stack of cash, making sure to get a receipt. Carrying an over-stuffed backpack, he walked into the shiny-floored terminal, and unpleasant memories flooded his head. Clivo had never flown in an airplane, as far as he could remember, at least, but he had spent plenty of time at the airport with Aunt Pearl, either dropping off or picking up his dad from his supposed archaeological digs. Clivo remembered all the sad goodbyes, Russell's promises to return as soon as he could—and the smell of airplane soap on Russell's hands when he finally did. Once again Clivo was awash in confusion as to why his dad had kept so many things a mystery.

Clivo pushed aside his thoughts and focused on getting a ticket. He scanned the counters, not sure which airline to fly, or even how to buy a ticket, so he picked a counter that was staffed by what seemed to be a nice attendant.

"Welcome to Pangaea Air, how can I help you today?" the chipper woman behind the counter asked. She had so much makeup on that her face was a different color from her neck.

"Hi, I need to fly to Portland, please," Clivo replied.

"Did you book a ticket online?" she asked pleasantly.

"Um, not this time," he said. *Next time, for sure.*

"Are you flying today, sir?" she asked.

Clivo tried not to laugh at being called "sir." "Yes, please."

"And which Portland, sir?" The woman looked at him expectantly as her nails clicked away at a furious pace on the keyboard.

Clivo pulled out the cryptozoology museum's business card and glanced at the address. "Um, Maine."

"How many tickets?"

"Just me."

The woman's fingers froze in midclick. "How old are you, sir?"

Clivo swallowed. "I'm eighteen. I'm just short. Still hoping for that growth spurt." He let out a little chuckle, but the woman kept her eyes trained on him.

"I'm going to need to see your ID, sir."

"Sure." Clivo pulled out his passport. He'd never traveled, but his dad had insisted he get it "in case of an emergency," whatever that meant. Clivo wasn't sure what kind of emergency would cause him to fly out of the country suddenly, but nothing much was making sense nowadays.

"It says you're thirteen here," the woman said, her sweet voice turning accusatory.

"Oh, does it? Well, I was adopted, and I guess my

parents got my birth date wrong." Clivo gave her a dimpled smile, hoping it would work on this woman the way it worked on Aunt Pearl.

The woman handed him back his passport. "Sorry, son, you need a parent or guardian to buy your ticket if you're that young."

As the next customer, a portly businessman with a sweaty face, crowded in behind him, Clivo had an idea. He whipped out his Diamond Card.

"Can I just buy a ticket with this, please? I have the money, at least I hope I do. I mean, money shouldn't be a problem, and I'm a really good flier. At least, I think I will be when I finally, you know, get to be on an airplane." Clivo flashed her another big, hopeful smile.

The woman looked at the Diamond Card and lifted her eyebrows so high her forehead makeup cracked. Even the guy behind him exclaimed, "Wow!"

"My deepest, sincerest apologies, esteemed sir. We have our daily flight to Portland leaving in an hour. Would you like coach, business, or first class?" The woman reverted to her chipper tone, her fingers resuming their frantic typing.

Clivo exhaled in relief. He was about to say coach when he caught himself. "Which do you recommend?"

"First class, of course." She leaned in closer and spoke in a whisper. "Never should a Diamond Cardholder fly coach."

"I'll take a seat in first class, then, please."

If Douglas was going to be yelling at him all the time anyway, Clivo figured he might as well give him something to yell about.

The woman nodded at him in approval. Clivo was worried the card wouldn't work or that a group of policemen would suddenly appear out of nowhere and tackle him to the ground for being an imposter. But the woman swiped the card, checked his bag, and handed him his boarding pass. Just when Clivo thought he was in the clear, the woman pressed a red button and a door was flung open behind her, revealing a scowling man—the biggest Clivo had ever seen. The man wore a dark suit that looked like it was about to split at the seams, and his shoulders were so muscular they swallowed his neck. He looked like a professional weight lifter and had one ginormous eyebrow that stretched across his whole forehead like a thick black caterpillar.

"Serge will accompany you through security, sir. Can we have a car waiting for you at the other end?"

"Sure," Clivo said absently, his voice rising a few octaves. He was transfixed by the monstrous man who was approaching him, blocking out the light from the overhead fluorescents.

"Perfect, sir. Have a lovely flight, and thank you for flying Pangaea Air."

IX

As it turned out, Clivo was glad to have burly Serge by his side going through security because Serge escorted him to a special lane for first-class passengers that had nobody waiting in line. The long line of grumpy coach passengers all scowled at him as he passed. He'd had no idea that he had to take off his shoes, belt, and sweatshirt before walking through some kind of x-ray body scanner. Serge was actually a really nice guy who spoke in a surprisingly high-pitched voice for someone so large.

"So, Serge, why am I getting such special treatment?" Clivo asked as he tied his shoes after going through security.

"Only VIPs have Diamond Cards," Serge said, his eyes swinging back and forth as if he expected someone to jump them. "Some of them are so important they're in danger of being kidnapped, so I make sure they get safely on the plane. I'm sorry, we didn't know you were coming or I would have met you outside."

"Oh, well, I'm not really an important person," Clivo said, hoping he wasn't in danger of being kidnapped.

"Your Diamond Card says otherwise," Serge said, gently putting his balloon-like fingers on Clivo's shoulder and leading him toward the gate. The terminal was crowded with people running for flights and smelled like Uncle Ernie's Buttery Pretzels.

Clivo thought about that. He certainly wasn't important, but maybe Douglas was. "So, what kind of people have Diamond Cards, anyway?"

Serge scratched his chin, which was as square and chiseled as a brick. "Oh you know, billionaires, movie stars, kings, sheiks, prime ministers. Then there are people like you, not as young as you, of course, who don't look like any of those. Those are the guys who work in government stuff."

"Government stuff?" Clivo asked.

"Yeah, you know, like undercover spies."

Clivo wondered if Douglas really was a spy. He definitely wasn't a movie star or a sheik. Maybe he was just a bored billionaire with nothing better to do than spend his money searching for the immortal cryptid.

"Well, I'm not any of those, so hopefully nobody will feel the need to kidnap me," Clivo said with a nervous laugh.

Serge looked at him, his fuzzy eyebrow crinkling with worry. "Like I said, Mr. Wren, if you have a Diamond Card, *someone* thinks you're important, which usually means someone else thinks you're dangerous, so watch your back."

Serge handed Clivo his boarding pass. "Here's your gate. I'll wait here to make sure the plane takes off safely, and your driver will be waiting for you in Portland. After that, be careful."

Clivo got on the plane, feeling nervous about Serge's warning. He knew he was racing the bad guys for the immortal cryptid, but he didn't think he'd actually come face-to-face with any of them.

Clivo's nervousness dissipated as he entered the first-class cabin. It really was the lap of luxury. At first he felt out of place in his cargo pants and oversized sweater while surrounded by businesspeople in fancy suits who stared at their computers as if their lives depended on it. But the perky flight attendants treated him like everyone else and gave him hot towels to wash his face with, a fancy breakfast of eggs and buttery croissants, and more juice than he could handle. He even asked for a third serving of the little foil-wrapped chocolates.

The five-hour flight went really quickly. Clivo spent the first hour looking out the window in awe at the fields and cities that passed below him in miniature scale. He watched dark rain clouds rise up in the distance and giggled as the plane bounced through some turbulence, because it made his belly feel like he was on a roller coaster. Finally, he reclined in his comfy seat and flipped through the hundreds of television, movie, shopping, and music channels offered on his own personal screen. The whole trip was so enjoyable that he was almost disappointed when the plane began its descent into southern Maine.

It was early evening by the time he arrived at the Portland International Jetport. Clivo followed the signs to the baggage-claim area. He descended on an escalator, and next to the flight's baggage carousel he saw a handsome young man in sunglasses holding a sign that said MR. C. WREN. The man was wearing a black leather jacket and stood with the straightest spine Clivo had ever seen.

"Hi, I'm Clivo Wren."

The man looked down his thin nose at Clivo, obviously expecting someone else. Probably someone older, without chocolate smeared all over his face.

"Run along, kid," the man said.

Clivo had learned his lesson at the ticket counter in Denver. He reached into his pocket, pulled out his wallet, and held up the Diamond Card.

The driver's manner changed instantly. "Excuse me, sir! My name is Nate. Follow me, please."

Now exuding eagerness, Nate picked up Clivo's backpack and led him into a waiting elevator discreetly located in a back corner of the large room. Inside, he pulled a key on a retractable chain from his pocket and inserted it into an unlabeled keyhole. He turned the key, pressed a button, and the elevator descended.

"Where are we going?" Clivo asked.

Nate had been silent the whole time, and after Serge's warning about Diamond Cardholders being kidnapped, Clivo was starting to wonder if he should have asked Nate for some sort of ID.

"To pick out your mode of transportation, sir."

"Oh, okay. Like a taxi or something?" Clivo asked, noticing that Nate's hair gel smelled distinctly like cauliflower soup.

Nate looked at him and laughed, as if Clivo had just made a joke. Clivo spent the rest of the ride in nervous silence.

The elevator opened into an underground parking garage, or, from Clivo's point of view, heaven. The concrete room was filled with fancy lighting and even fancier cars. They were lined up neatly in slanted rows, the lights glinting off the spotless metal and chrome. Clivo had never thought he'd see cars like this in person, never mind in a private showroom. There was even a pair of motorcycles along the far wall.

Clivo looked, bug-eyed, at Nate, who gave him a wink.

"Time to choose your future, young man," he said.

"From . . . these?" Clivo asked, barely able to speak.

"Reserved for Diamond Cardholders only. Today we have the Ferrari 812 Superfast, an Aston Martin Vantage, and the Porsche—"

"A Porsche 918 Spyder," Clivo said.

"That's right. I apologize that the Lamborghini is out

of service today . . . A client came through just yesterday and took a drive along the Maine coast a little too fast and furiously." Nate chuckled at his little joke. "But I hope something else here can suffice."

Clivo nodded, unable to tear his eyes from the embarrassment of riches in front of him. Douglas definitely hadn't said anything about *not* renting a luxury sports car, Clivo reasoned. He scanned the room, and it took him just a moment to decide. "The Spyder. I'll go with the Porsche 918 Spyder, please."

Nate took a deep breath and placed his hand on Clivo's shoulder in a congratulatory gesture. "Your taste is exquisite."

Minutes later, Nate squealed the silver convertible out of the parking garage with Clivo strapped into the passenger seat. Once again Clivo was certain that a gang of policemen was going to appear out of nowhere and pull them over for impersonating a VIP. But his fear was overpowered by the elated smile plastered to his face.

When Clivo had told Nate his destination, the young driver gave him the news that the International Cryptozoology Museum was no more than a ten-minute drive from the airport. Clivo had been hoping for at least an hour's joyride.

"Unless you are not in a rush," Nate prompted, obviously noting the crestfallen look on Clivo's face.

"Well, the museum only seems to be open at night, so I might have a little time to kill," Clivo said.

With that, Nate powered them smoothly up and down winding roads along the Atlantic coastline north of the city before whipping back to town on a divided highway. It was an overcast evening, and for the first time in his life Clivo smelled the ocean. It was sweet and salty and gave him a yearning for clam chowder that didn't come from a can.

He mentioned this to Nate, who said he knew just the place. At a fish shack beside a little cove Clivo tasted the creamy goodness of real New England clam chowder and gobbled his first lobster roll, then immediately ordered a second. Thus far, the life of a cryptid catcher wasn't too bad.

His stomach was full and the sky was pitch-dark by the time they pulled up outside the cryptozoology museum, where a light was burning brightly over the entrance.

"I may be in here for a while; is that okay?" Clivo asked Nate.

"I could spend the rest of my days in this Porsche and ask nothing more from life," Nate said, lovingly stroking the leather steering wheel.

Clivo assumed that meant it was fine.

The museum was a two-story brick building and advertised itself with a hanging sign depicting a tusk-toothed fish. Clivo entered, paid the seven-dollar admission to the enthusiastic cashier, and walked into a crypto wonderland. He seemed to have the place to himself.

The walls and display cases were filled with information about every cryptid imaginable. Fur supposedly from the Yeti sat in one case, plaster footprints of a Loveland frogman sat in another, and all the famous photographs of Nessie, the Loch Ness Monster, were displayed in one corner.

There was even a tiny movie theater where video footage of purported cryptid sightings was playing. Blurry images of Bigfoot and Nessie danced on the wall, though most of them were comical. The Bigfoot sightings were obviously people in gorilla suits (one with a visible price tag still on it), and one sighting of Nessie was clearly a sailboat with a fake dinosaur head on its mast.

Clivo spent a half hour reading the identification cards at as many exhibits as he could. The information was interesting, and some of it was downright entertaining, especially the firsthand accounts of people who made ridiculous claims. One woman claimed that she was the Feejee mermaid but would only transform if nobody was looking, and another guy claimed the Jersey Devil was really his mother-in-law.

When Clivo's eyes began to sting from so much reading, he realized that none of it told him *exactly* where to find a cryptid. His dad must have had more information to go on.

"Excuse me," Clivo said, startling the young teenage cashier, who was engrossed in a comic book.

"Sorry. What can I help you with, dude?" he asked, quickly closing the comic and placing it beneath the register. His name tag said CHARLES and he looked like a kid from the '70s, down to the curly blond hair and faded Izod shirt. His buck teeth made him look like an angry rabbit.

"This is going to sound kind of strange," Clivo began.

"Please, you're standing in front of a skunk-monkey; everything is strange in here," Charles said, waving his hand as if shooing away a bee.

"Okay, well, I've read a lot of the exhibits, but I'm looking for more specific information. Like exactly where to find a cryptid."

"Oh, that's easy," Charles said, once again waving his hand in front of him. "For Bigfoot over there, just head to the forests of the Pacific Northwest and look for its scat. There's tons of it everywhere. Like, that guy must just eat and poop all day."

"Wow, okay. What else?"

"That guy over there. The chupacabra." Charles pointed to a drawing of what looked like a kangaroo mixed with a lizard. Clivo's stomach dropped when he saw its sharp claws. He imagined his dad fighting with the creature, but quickly shoved the image out of his mind. "It's only been seen since around 1995, so it's more of a contemporary cryptid, with the first sightings coming out of Puerto Rico. Go there and look for dead goats. It's known for being a goatsucker, and they've found tons, I mean *piles*, of goats just sucked dry. Like this thing just sticks a straw in them and sucks the blood out like a milk shake."

Charles puckered his lips and made a loud sucking noise, making his eyes wide to emphasize the point. A couple with a loud kid who had wandered in as Clivo was browsing exited the museum just then, looks of disgust on their faces.

"Oh, hey, thanks for coming! Does your kid want a lollipop? No? Okay, hope to see you again soon," Charles called to them, putting down a sucker that he had grabbed from below the counter. "Anyway, yeah, to find a chup, look for the goats. There's no way a human could drain that much blood that quickly. I mean, unless you're Dracula, but that dude lives in Transylvania. Too much sun in Puerto Rico. Ha! Could you imagine the count with a tan! That's just so wrong!" Charles let out a laugh that sounded halfway between a bark and a snort.

Clivo politely joined him in the laugh. "That's interesting stuff, definitely. Anything else?"

"Yeah, only the *mother ship*. The big kahuna of cryptids. The one that I'd give my comics collection to see. I'm talking about the Abominable. The Yeti. The wicked snow dweller in the Himalayas. That dude is nothing less than *prehistoric*. And way remote. Sir Edmund Hillary saw its tracks while climbing the tallest mountain in the world, Everest. That Yeti dude is fierce—it survives in frigid temperatures where absolutely nothing grows."

"So what does it eat?" Clivo asked out of genuine curiosity.

"It, like, eats whatever it wants! It probably devours the climbers that don't make it down from Everest. You know their corpses are just left to freeze up there, right? When you climb up, the route takes you past all sorts of dead climbers from decades ago."

"No, I didn't know that," Clivo replied, making a mental note to never climb Everest.

"Totally! So, like, right now, if I were to climb Everest, which I totally could 'cause I run track, I would see just like a highway of frozen bodies all the way up."

"Or maybe you wouldn't since the Yeti would've eaten them," Clivo offered.

Charles snort-barked again.

"Right? That's what I'm saying! Dude is so cool."

Clivo would have asked for more information on the Yeti, but searching for a flesh-eating monster in a blizzard sounded horrible, to say the least.

"Any others that might be a bit less . . . dangerous?" Clivo asked.

"Well, sure. If you need a creature that won't try to eat your face off, I recommend Nessie."

"The Loch Ness Monster?" That sounded good to Clivo. A gentle manatee-like creature that floated in a lake. Much better.

"Oh, yeah. I didn't mention her because she's kinda the obvious one. And pretty boring, if you ask me," Charles said, rubbing his nose. "Everybody and their mother have been going to Scotland for decades trying to find her."

"So if I were to go to Scotland and look for her, do you know how I could find her? I mean, *exactly* where to look and stuff?"

That shut Charles up like a Venus flytrap snagging its dinner. "You sure do ask a lot of questions," he said, leaning back and crossing his arms.

"Oh. Well, I thought that, this being a museum and all . . ."

"That info's not included in the price of admission, buddy."

"No problem, I can totally pay." Clivo pulled out the Diamond Card and slid it across the counter. The tactic had worked for him so far.

But Charles barely glanced at the card and seemed completely unimpressed. He narrowed his eyes. "Password?"

"Password?"

"Pass. Word." Charles clearly enunciated both syllables.

The kid seemed to know other information that might be useful, but he obviously wasn't giving it up without the password. Clivo wondered if maybe this was why his dad had taught him other languages?

"Um, *pomogite*?" Clivo offered, saying "help" in Russian.

"What?" Charles asked, wrinkling his nose.

"Tasuke?" Clivo continued, trying it in Japanese.

"Huh?"

Clivo tried Arabic and Hindustani, but Charles just looked at him like he was losing his marbles.

Clivo racked his brain about where his dad might have kept the password before realizing the obvious. He pulled out his wallet to check the museum's business card.

"Cyborg?"

Charles's eyes snapped to him. They narrowed again, but he nodded in begrudging acceptance. "Put your arms out to your sides," Charles commanded, stepping from behind the counter.

"What for?"

"I have to pat you down for weapons."

Clivo let out a laugh before noticing the no-fooling expression on Charles's face. "Oh. Are you being serious?"

"Dude, just let me pat you down, okay? It's part of the code."

Clivo put his arms out to his sides as Charles patted

him down. Not that Clivo had ever been through a pat-down before, but he was pretty sure this was a poor excuse for one.

"Just checking to see if you're packing any heat. Not that that'd worry me. I take karate." Charles put his hands together and gave a little bow. "I could totally take you out with one hand."

By way of example, he quickly punched a hand toward Clivo's face. Without thinking, Clivo blocked it and twisted Charles's arm behind his back as he swung him around, slamming his body onto the countertop.

"Foliage! Foliage!" Charles squealed.

"What?" Clivo asked. His body had reacted so quickly to the attack that he wasn't even sure what had just happened.

"It's the safe word I use in karate class. It means 'Let me go, man!'"

Clivo released Charles, who stood up and rubbed his shoulder with a pained expression.

"Dang, I was just going to give an example," Charles complained. "You didn't have to go all Green Beret on me."

"I'm really sorry. I do jujitsu. I guess it's a bit instinctual at this point," Clivo apologized.

"Yeah, well, I run track but it doesn't mean I hurdle everything I see," Charles said, still rubbing his shoulder and eyeing Clivo sideways as he retreated back behind the counter.

Charles pulled a notebook from under the counter and opened it to a page that read *The Beast of Bradford Mountain*. Below it was a drawing of a massive Bigfoot-like creature with glowing red eyes and extremely hairy knuckles. "We haven't had time to put up an official exhibit yet 'cause the sightings for this guy are pretty new. There was a report just last night, actually. If you're interested, we could sure use your help verifying its existence."

Clivo swallowed. "It looks pretty vicious."

"Very," Charles said with foreboding. "If you're not careful it'll suck your brain out right through your ears."

Clivo winced as Charles made another loud sucking sound through his buck teeth. "Is there maybe another cryptid around here that won't do that?"

Charles slammed the notebook shut and put it away. "You wanted information about where to find a cryptid; I gave it to you. Now, are you interested in helping out or not?"

Clivo's long, cross-country day was beginning to catch up with him. He was more interested in having Nate take him to a cheap motel where he could crash for the night, but it sounded like he'd stumbled onto his very first cryptid-catching opportunity, and he didn't want to miss the boat.

"I'll do it," Clivo said. "Just tell me where I need to go."

Charles gave him directions to a park on the north side

of the city and drew him a little map with the exact path to follow once he was there.

"Good luck, dude," he said.

Clivo headed out the door, realizing that life as a cryptid catcher had just become a lot more dangerous.

X

Clivo exited the museum and climbed inside the Porsche, which was still parked right out front. He gave Nate directions to the park, grateful that the driver didn't ask why he wanted to go there in the dark of night, way after the park's closing time. Instead, Nate seemed excited to have more driving to do.

They drove to Bradford Mountain, and this time Clivo asked Nate to drop him off in the empty parking lot and leave. He had no idea how long it would take to catch his first cryptid, and he didn't want Nate to get worried and come looking for him right as he tranquilized the Beast.

To a kid raised in the Rockies, Bradford Mountain seemed more like a molehill than a mountain, from what Clivo could tell in the gloom. He grabbed his backpack with the tranquilizer gun and blood sampler and headed to a dirt pathway. The forest was dense, with tall trees so packed together that the trail quickly disappeared into shadow. Thick patches of scrubby plants blanketed the forest floor, making the place feel very lush, but also incredibly spooky. An owl hooted overhead, as if in warning not to go in.

"Okay, all you have to do is walk into this incredibly creepy deserted forest and find a beast that wants to eat your head. Piece of cake," Clivo mumbled.

He took a deep breath and entered the dark forest, his skin rising with goose bumps even though the air was warm and humid. He walked slowly, all of his senses sharp for any sight or sound around him. A few night birds chirped overhead, and there was the occasional scurry of something in the underbrush, but all in all the forest was quiet, save for Clivo's racing heartbeat, which pounded like a gong in his head.

Russell had taken him animal tracking many times in the Rockies, though Clivo had never understood why. They'd track a deer or a moose, sometimes for hours, and once they spotted it, Clivo would see how close he could get to the animal before it discovered him and ran away. He'd always thought it was pretty fun, and spending time with his dad was the best, but now he understood it had been more than a game; it was part of his training for finding cryptids.

Clivo realized that that training would probably come in handy right about then, and he focused his attention on the dirt path in front of him, looking for any animal tracks that would direct him toward the Beast of Bradford Mountain that lurked in the trees. He quickly noticed footprints and paw prints of all sizes, but nothing that looked like some unknown creature. After wandering up and down the main trail and several smaller offshoots, he was ready to give up. Then he rounded a sharp bend and saw a print right in the middle of the path that most definitely belonged to a beast. It was twice as big as any human print, but what really gave it away were the two massive toes that split the foot apart like a hoof. Whatever this thing was, it was enormous.

Clivo swallowed but kept on, doing his best to track the prints. But there was only the one. Either the Beast had just disappeared or its footsteps were too far apart to track. So he continued forward, really not liking the feeling that he was the prey and not the hunter.

He was moving through the pitch-black forest when a growl sounded to his right. Clivo immediately froze, out of both fear and instinct. He turned his head as slowly as possible toward the noise, terrified of the monster he knew he was about to see.

But no creature sprang out at him. Clivo stood stiffly, trying to stifle his loud breathing, and scanned the spaces between the shadowy leaves and branches. Nothing was there, and no other growls sounded from the bush.

Clivo relaxed his shoulders, figuring he'd imagined the sound, and continued on his way, his feet moving as quickly and silently as possible.

After another fifteen minutes of walking with his head

whipping back and forth at the slightest rustling in the bushes and trees, he saw a clearing lit with moonlight. At least he could get out of the pitch-blackness of the forest for a moment . . .

Clivo froze again as a growl—and it was most definitely a growl, low and deep—sounded right next to him. He swiveled his head toward the noise and was pretty sure his heart came to a complete standstill as a pair of red eyes glowed from the bushes beside him.

"Shoot," Clivo murmured.

He dropped to his knees and slowly crawled backward into the brush, where he hid on his belly, keeping his eyes on the red glow. But nothing more happened. There was no rustling of shrubbery, no further growls, and the red eyes blinked out like a light.

Moving as silently as possible, he pulled out the case with the tranquilizer gun and darts. There were about ten darts, and they came in different sizes, probably depending on the size of the cryptid being captured. At the base of each needle was a glass bubble with a yellowish viscous liquid inside.

He chose the largest dart and fitted it in the gun, listening for any more beast noises. After a moment another growl sounded, but it was farther down the path. Clivo couldn't believe he was making the decision to go *toward* a deadly creature, but he was eager to have his first catch under his belt. He wanted to prove to Douglas—and to himself—that he could actually do this. He held his gun with shaking hands and silently went in pursuit.

He reached the open clearing and barely had a moment to get his bearings when another growl shattered the peaceful scene and a pair of red eyes appeared to his right. He didn't hesitate; he swept down to his knees and fired the gun directly toward the creature. The tranq gun clicked, but nothing happened.

"Come on," Clivo mumbled, clicking off the safety latch.

He aimed and fired again, the dart finding its mark. But instead of a thud and some sort of zombie squeal like he was expecting, a metallic thwack sounded and a shower of sparks exploded in the air.

Before Clivo could guess what was going on, a hairy creature stumbled from the brush and ran straight toward him. It was short—shorter than Clivo—but had impossibly long, shaggy arms that reached toward him as a roar pierced the air.

Clivo ducked and tripped the creature, causing it to fly forward with a wail of shock. Clivo jumped on it, not really sure what he was doing, but he figured he'd better wrestle with the Beast while he had the element of surprise in his favor.

He had raised his fist to deliver a solid punch when the creature squealed in a young voice, "Klondike Bar! Klondike Bar!"

"What?" Clivo asked. He had been too panicked to notice that his assailant was hardly putting up a fight.

"That's his safe word, man! Let him go!" another voice yelled as a figure bolted from the trees.

Clivo released his attacker just as Charles ran up, a smoldering toy robot in his hands.

"Hernando! I warned you not to do that! I told you he'd go all Green Beret on you. And you"—he pointed a stabbing finger at Clivo—"what's with shooting my robot?"

"Oh, sorry," Clivo replied, trying to calm his breath. "I was trying to tranquilize the Beast. What are you guys doing here?"

"Ha-ha! The Beast doesn't exist, dude!" Charles waved a walkie-talkie that emitted the scary growling sound. "Oldest trick in the book!"

Hernando, a pudgy kid Clivo's age, crawled to his feet. He shook off his costume, which was simply an oversized fur coat with broomsticks in the sleeves to make them extra long. "Congratulations. Nobody's ever tackled me before," he said meekly. "Usually people go screaming in terror at the first growl."

"Don't give him that much credit, it's not like he faced an actual cryptid," Charles pointed out.

Clivo finally caught his breath, his racing heartbeat returning to normal. "Was this an initiation or something?"

"Obviously, dude." Charles snorted. "Every top secret club has an initiation to weed out the unworthy ones."

"Very unworthy," Hernando agreed.

"Did I pass?" Clivo asked hopefully.

"I guess so." Charles shrugged. "Just don't let it go to your head. Now, put that gun away! You're holding it like an amateur."

Clivo secured the gun in his backpack and the three boys walked down the long path to the main road, where they caught a city bus that wound them away from the park and eventually into a nice residential neighborhood.

Charles sat across the aisle from Clivo with his arms crossed and a scowl on his face, whereas Hernando clasped his hands in his lap and observed Clivo with a pleasant smile.

They exited the bus in front of a pale-blue house and Charles led them around the back, where they descended some concrete stairs into a basement doorway.

Clivo followed Charles into the house and felt like he had just entered a crypto fantasyland. The large room was unlit except for a string of white Christmas lights and vanilla-scented candles that cast a mysterious glow around the space. Teetering wooden bookcases crammed with books of all sizes leaned against the walls, and small figurines of cryptids dangled from the ceiling on strings. Multicolored fabrics were strung from the ceiling as well, making the place feel like a tent. Battered old wall maps hung next to a frayed fire-breathing dragon poster that read IF YOU CAN'T STAND THE HEAT, GET OUT OF THE DUNGEON. Several wooden desks were crowded into the corners, and all were lit by what looked to be old oil wick lanterns. Between the candles and the lanterns and the exotic drapery, the place was a fire hazard for sure, but the dim lighting certainly created the feeling of a secret headquarters.

Scattered around the room, sitting on sofas or beanbag chairs, were several kids who looked roughly Clivo's age, their faces lit by the glow of laptops. They stared at him with mouths open in surprise.

"Dude, why isn't he blindfolded?" a kid on a red beanbag chair asked. It was hard to tell with him sitting down, but he looked to be really gangly and thin, with a pair of glasses that Jerry would have referred to as "single-forever glasses" because there was no way anyone could get a girlfriend with such big, ugly frames.

"He passed the initiation, Adam, no thanks to Hernando's poor fighting skills," Charles replied, pointing an accusing finger at Hernando.

"I had to use my safe word," Hernando said quietly.

"But now he's seen our faces, dumbwad!" Adam yelled.

"Then you try blindfolding him, goggle breath, and see how you like getting tackled!" Charles retorted.

Clivo had no idea what kind of motley crew he had stumbled upon, but it was definitely not the shadowy, grim group he'd been expecting. These kids couldn't have been the people his dad had gotten his information from, but maybe they could tell him something of use. Seeing as how he knew absolutely nothing, any piece of information would be helpful.

Adam got up from his seat and sauntered over until he was standing nose to nose with Clivo.

"You with McConaughey's clan?" Adam sucked his top teeth with his bottom lip as if he was in some kind of Old West standoff.

"Uh, no."

"So you're not with McConaughey?"

"Who's McConaughey?"

"You look like you're with McConaughey."

Clivo looked to Charles. "Help?"

"McConaughey is a fellow cryptozoologist," Charles said, stepping between them. "Lives over in Vermont. He wants to join forces, but the guy couldn't find a unicorn if he sat on its horn. Now he keeps sending moles to infiltrate our headquarters and steal our intel."

Adam cracked his knuckles.

"It's a major turf war, man. Major."

Clivo laughed, but clamped his mouth shut when he saw their serious expressions. "You mean, you guys actually have crypto turf wars?"

"Darn straight," Adam said. "They keep trying to impress people in the chat rooms with data they steal from us. But we got back at 'em."

"How did you do that?" Clivo asked, curious how

conspiracy groups went to battle. Maybe they stood in a field and threw flash drives at each other.

"Just by . . . jeez . . . you know, e-mailing them that that's not cool and stuff and not to do that kind of thing," Charles said.

"Don't do that," Hernando agreed, wagging a finger back and forth.

Adam stepped around Charles so he could point his big nose at Clivo's face. Clivo wished he would stop doing that—his breath smelled worse than Jerry's dog Hercules's did.

"But you passed our terrifying initiation, so I guess you're cool. Just don't test me, or you'll regret it."

"You'll be full of regrets," Hernando softly agreed.

Clivo was so busy squinting away from Adam's invasive face that he barely noticed the girls in the room until they spoke.

"Don't pay attention to Adam. He's trying to wean himself off of Ritalin, so he's a bit high-strung right now. Welcome to our club; we call ourselves the Myth Blasters. We research the existence of creatures that appear in legends and literature and have first-person visual accounts but have never been officially recognized by science," said a girl with golden hair tucked into a knot on her head. She blushed furiously, accentuating her slight case of acne.

"That's a pretty intense after-school club," Clivo replied.

He noticed that the girl was really pretty, with the lightest-blue eyes he had ever seen.

A short, brown-skinned girl with a pierced nose stood up from a chair.

"Yeah, we tried the drama club. Wasn't really our speed. Too much enthusiasm."

Charles introduced the girls with a sigh.

"Clivo, this is Stephanie and Amelia. We tried to keep Myth Blasters an all-boys club, but Stephanie's parents let us use their basement for headquarters, so we kinda had to let her join. And you know girls, they always have to do things together, hence the Amelia presence."

Stephanie blushed again. "They were meeting at a Taco Comet before, so this place was really a step up."

"And their research methods were crap until we sorted them out, so that's a bonus, too," Amelia added.

Clivo sneezed. The scented candles were overpowering, and Adam was doused in some kind of strong cologne. "So you guys actually believe that legendary animals exist?"

"No, we don't believe they exist." Amelia sighed.

"Oh."

"We *know* they exist."

"What do you mean? Like you have proof?"

Amelia eyed him. "Of course we have proof. We're the only group, at least in the Lower Forty-Eight, that does."

"Why do you think McConaughey is up in our grill all the time?" Adam sneered.

"So, you've actually found one? You've found a legendary creature?" Clivo was having a hard time believing that this group knew anything beyond the usual theories and discoveries. They were kids in a basement on laptops, how much could they possibly know? Clivo made a mental note to check with McConaughey in Vermont in case he could provide any better help.

Amelia blew through her lips.

"Find one? Let's see, I'm a middle-schooler who works at the local bookstore ten hours a week for less than minimum wage. Yeah, that should totally cover the cost of a plane ticket, hotel, and crypto-research manual."

"What's a crypto-research manual?" Clivo asked.

Adam held up his hands to stop anyone from speaking.

"Hang on, hang on. Now listen here, tough guy, you come in here with your good-looking dimples and thick head of hair and think you can just flirt with the women—"

"The women," Hernando quietly concurred.

"And you gain access to our secure fortress by passing an un-passable initiation, yet you pretend to know very little about what it is we actually do. Just casually fishing for information, are you? Well, think again, scummy spy! Boys, get him!"

Adam pointed, as if fully expecting Charles and

Hernando to rush Clivo. But the two boys held their ground. If anything, they backed up a few steps.

Adam grunted with frustration and rushed Clivo himself. Clivo instinctually took a crouching stance, both hands in a striking pose, once again his body responding of its own accord. Adam immediately stopped a few steps away and bounced up and down, like a boxer preparing for a fight.

"Someone give him some Ritalin," Amelia said with a groan.

Adam did a few fake punches, making odd yelling noises as he did so. Clivo didn't recognize any of the moves and wondered if Adam actually knew any martial arts. Then Adam finally made his charge, attempting to punch and grab Clivo at the same time. Clivo quickly stepped aside and tripped the kid, who did a spectacular fall face-first into a beanbag chair.

"Luke, I am your father," Adam said, his voice muffled by the stuffing.

"Are those his safe words?" Clivo asked.

Charles nodded. "It's a bit long, but he insists on it."

Before anyone could tackle him again, Clivo reached into his wallet and pulled out a picture of his mom and dad. The photo was old and faded, but he kept it because he had always thought his mom looked beautiful in it, her face aglow from the sunset on top of Lookout Mountain near their home.

"You're right, I don't know anything about what you guys do. I found out about you from my dad."

Stephanie took the photo in her delicate fingers. "Russell Wren is your dad?"

"You know him?" Clivo asked, surprised that Stephanie knew his father's name.

"Sure. He was actually supposed to be here a while ago to buy another crypto-research manual, but he never showed up. Is everything okay?"

Clivo carefully put the crinkled photo back into his wallet. "My dad's gone. He died, suddenly, a few months ago."

Exclamations of disbelief rumbled through the rest of the group.

"I'm so, so sorry!" Stephanie said. Tears sprang to her eyes.

"That sucks big toes, man," Adam said, pushing himself to his feet.

"He was a super-nice guy, dude," Charles added.

"A good man," Hernando agreed, blowing his nose into a handkerchief.

"Thanks," Clivo said, swallowing the lump that was rising in his throat. "So, can I ask what my dad came here for?"

"Information," Amelia said, her voice somber. "He wanted our research about where to find certain cryptids."

"He came to *you* guys for information?" Clivo asked, even more surprised.

"Why the shock?" Adam practically yelled. "Who else is he gonna go to? The Bigger Bigfoot Search Party? They couldn't help him find the back of his hand."

"No, no shock," Clivo assured them. "I'm just having a hard time adjusting to whatever planet I've landed on. Anyway, did you give him any information?"

Amelia nodded. "We told him where to find the Honey Island Swamp Monster, a blue tiger, and a chupacabra."

Clivo froze. His father had found all of those creatures. Either it was coincidence, or these kids really were as good as they said they were. Clivo asked the next question carefully. "What did my dad tell you about what he did?"

Charles thought about it. "Not much. Just that he was an archaeologist who traveled the world going on digs. He liked learning about the mythology of an area while he was stuck there dusting off bones. Said it was a fun hobby, the possibility of finding a living relic while digging for dead ones."

"And did he tell you if he found any cryptids?" Clivo asked, a pang of jealousy hitting him at the thought that his father had revealed his secrets to these kids, but never to him.

"Nah. He said he thought he came close a few times, though. Maybe saw some blue tiger scat," Charles said.

Clivo felt oddly relieved. At least he wasn't the only person his dad had lied to. "So, if you guys are so protective of your information, why did you give it to my dad?"

This time Stephanie answered, her face blotchy from crying. "Well, he was a really nice guy. He paid us a little bit for our work. But our reasons were more selfish."

"Selfish?"

"Sure. We really believe that these legendary animals are out there. We know where they are, we just don't have the means to actually find them. Your dad had the ability to do all that. He could travel the world and do the searching, with our information as his guide. It was perfect. He was like our own field agent."

"And he brought us pizza," Hernando added.

"And he promised that anything he found, we would get the credit for," Adam said. "Suck on that, McConaughey!"

Clivo wished he could bring out his dad's cryptid photo album and show it to these guys—they deserved to know that their research had been right. But if his dad hadn't told them anything, he figured he probably shouldn't, either.

"So, with my dad gone, it sounds like you guys need a new field agent. Would you be okay working with me?" Clivo tried to keep his voice casual, hoping they wouldn't notice how desperate he was for their help.

Stephanie looked confused. "I don't understand. You're a bit young to be an archaeologist. How can you be our field agent?"

Clivo stared at the group for an uncomfortable amount of time, his mind trying to come up with a believable cover story. Adam began tapping his foot impatiently. "Uh, my dad died without ever finding a cryptid," he began slowly, carefully crafting his lie. "He left me some money so I could keep looking. As a means to honor his memory, I suppose. He came to you guys for a reason—"

" 'Cause we're the best," Adam interjected.

"So if I'm really going to find a cryptid, I think I'd better stick to working with you." At least the last part felt true.

The gang all looked at each other, their faces sparked with excitement. One by one they nodded in agreement.

"You've come to the right place, Clivo Wren, son of Russell," Amelia said. "Now, where would you like to begin?"

XI

Half an hour later, Clivo was sitting on a beanbag chair in front of a digital projector, watching a PowerPoint presentation on Nessie. Amelia clicked through the photos, some in color and others in grainy black-and-white.

"We've sifted through all three thousand documented photographs and deemed seventy of them to be real. That is, actual photos of Nessie and not fake ones using toy boats and figurines." Amelia sounded like a stuffy professor giving a lecture.

"How did you do that?" Clivo asked, already amazed by the smarts of the group.

"That'd be me," Charles said, raising his hand. "Most are easy to debunk. You just look at forced perspective, examine shadows on the water, pixilate the images, and look for inconsistencies, etcetera. Others are a little trickier, but nothing a night of Moxie soda and energy drinks and Cheez-Its can't handle."

Amelia pointed a red laser dot at Charles's chest.

"Charles is our film and photography expert. Show him any photo or video and he can verify its authenticity within a day."

"Within a minute, yo. And don't point that thing at me! It freaks me out, like a sniper's got a rifle pointed at my chest." Charles tried to wave the red dot away from him.

"Have you ever *had* a sniper's weapon pointed at your chest?" Clivo asked, a bit curious. Ever since he'd discovered that aliens and other cryptids really did exist, his orientation as to what was and wasn't possible in the world had been majorly out of whack.

"Dude, when you know the stuff that we know, it's just a matter of time."

Clivo wasn't sure about that, but Charles's intense angry-rabbit look was very convincing.

Amelia clicked the control and hand-drawn pictures of Nessie glowed on the screen. The monster looked like a long serpent with multiple humps sprouting out of the water.

"Next up, going through literature and finding stories, no matter how obscure, that reference the cryptid. Legends always have some grain of truth to them. There are very few that are just pure fabrication." Amelia grabbed a flashlight and placed it under her chin, giving her face a ghostly glow. "That's my department. I found over two hundred references to a sea monster in the loch, going all the way back to the first century AD, well before she was documented by photo."

"But I thought cryptozoology and mythozoology were two totally separate things," Clivo said.

Adam groaned. "Let me guess, you were on IMyths ThePast.com. Those guys are so boring."

"They kind of are separate things," Amelia continued. "Cryptids are animals from folklore that may actually exist, it just hasn't been proven yet. Myths are stories created to explain the world around us, and they sometimes include gods and magical creatures. Now, most people don't believe mythological beings actually exist. Nobody has seen Zeus, Medusa, or the Minotaur, or at least there are no reliable accounts in the modern historical record. But if we did have a sighting of them, they'd be considered a cryptid. At least according to us."

"And we'd be after them like stink on a monkey," Adam said, popping some grapes into his mouth.

Clivo looked around in disbelief. He was officially stepping into territory that made his brain hurt. "You don't actually believe in *Zeus*, do you?"

Amelia shrugged. "We're more science based. We don't discount the possibility that he exists, but we focus our attention on things that have more data attached to them."

Clivo opened his mouth, then shut it again. Aliens and Bigfoot were about all he could handle right now. Contemplating the existence of gods would have to wait.

Amelia clicked her control again and what looked to be satellite photos of the loch sprang onto the screen.

Clivo leaned forward in amazement, or as much as he could lean forward while sitting on a beanbag chair.

"Are those satellite photos?"

"Sure are. Miss Hacker over here was able to break into a private satellite and steal a peek from above. As you can see, we found a shape in the water that matches the size and description of Nessie, even with the poor resolution."

Stephanie spoke next. She was eager but timid, like a mouse delicately sniffing a delicious piece of cheese.

"I was only able to gain control of the satellite for a few minutes before I was bumped off. But I'm hoping to increase my time and, someday, get into a government spy satellite. Their visual precision is incredible. I could zoom in from six hundred miles above Earth and tell if you're wearing contacts. Which you're not." She suddenly blushed and averted her eyes, which had been gazing intently into Clivo's.

"Wait, you can hack *satellites*?" Clivo's respect for the group was going through the roof.

"This presentation will go a lot faster if you keep your constant expressions of amazement to a minimum," Adam offered.

Clivo made a zipper motion with his fingers across his lips.

The screen clicked again and again, showing pictures

137

of boats trawling the loch with various nets and sonar equipment.

Amelia continued, "Hernando here is our information sifter. He takes everything that Charles, Stephanie, and I find and makes sense of it all. Triangulates coordinates, that kind of thing."

Hernando cleared his throat. "Can I have the laser, please?"

"Huh? Oh sure, sorry about that, Hernando." Amelia pointed the red laser at his chest. "He also researches previous attempts to find said cryptids and gathers their data."

Amelia turned off the laser and rubbed her hands together.

"So, once we've done all of that, we usually have a pretty good idea if the cryptid is real or not and where to find it."

Clivo scratched his head. He had so many questions he wasn't sure where to begin. "So why hasn't anybody found Nessie? If there have been so many searches, it seems like somebody would have found her by now."

For the first time Amelia seemed hesitant and uncertain. "Ah, that's the mystery now, isn't it? They're not called 'hidden animals' for nothing. Every cryptid is a singular, unique creature that has adapted to avoid detection, sometimes for centuries. They are rare evolutionary mutations that have survived specifically *because* they haven't been found. But, just as each cryptid is unique in its evolutionary development, it's also unique in its ability to hide."

"Unique in its ability to hide?"

"Perhaps they're invisible or really good at camouflaging themselves. It's different for each creature. We know they're there—the data are sound—they're just super hard to find."

"So how *do* you find them?" Clivo asked.

Stephanie leaned in again, her brow furrowing. "We actually don't know. That'll be your job to figure out."

A voice emanated from the other corner of the room.

"I've been waiting patiently over here, people," Adam said, waving his arms dramatically.

Amelia flipped to the next slide, which showed a maniacally smiling Adam wearing lab safety goggles and holding two flaming glass beakers. Amelia sighed.

"Sorry, he wanted a rather dramatic photo."

Adam unfolded his gangly limbs and stood up from his chair. "To wrap up this rather dry yet informative session, yours truly figures out how the animal evolved. Like how Peter Parker became Spider-Man. I deduce its origin story."

"Origin story? Like, where it was born?" Clivo asked.

"Not *where* it was born, but *how* it was born," Amelia

said. "It's possible it was born as it exists today, but it's more likely it morphed into what it is due to some event."

"Like Peter Parker getting bitten by a radioactive spider: Whammo! We have Spider-Man! Best origin story ever!" Adam interjected.

"Dude! Not even! Captain Marvel is. An ancient wizard named Shazam bequeathing you a lightning bolt is so much better," Charles argued.

"I'm not getting into this with you, dude!" Adam yelled.

Amelia rolled her eyes and continued. "Keep in mind, most cryptids are hundreds, if not thousands of years old. That's impossible, unless something cataclysmic happened to cause an anomaly in their biology."

"Moving along," Adam said, "once I figure out the origin story, I deduce how they hide. With Nessie, we think she's evolved to camouflage herself so thoroughly she can basically become invisible. It's the only plausible reason for why she can exist in an enclosed body of water, completely surrounded by humans yet seen by so few people."

Charles nodded. "As Sherlock Holmes said, 'When you have eliminated the impossible, whatever remains, however improbable, must be the truth.'"

Clivo shook his head in awe. "How did you guys come up with all this?"

Amelia turned off the projector and flipped on some

lights. "We all go to a magnet school for kids with freaky-deaky intelligence. While you were learning long division, we were mastering trig and calculus. Or while you were pondering the rather obvious metaphors in *Animal Farm*, we were reading Shakespeare's canon."

"Which Amelia proved was actually written by Shakespeare's plumber," Stephanie said proudly.

"Not even a challenge," Amelia said with a sniff.

"I just have one more question," Clivo said, standing up from his beanbag chair, which was cramping his legs. And who was he kidding? He had tons of questions. "People *have* seen cryptids, otherwise their legends wouldn't exist. How did that happen?"

"Unless the cryptid is totally invisible, it's not out of the realm of possibility that a human would accidentally come across one," Amelia said. "But they learn how not to be seen. Take sea monsters, like the Kraken. When ships used to cross the ocean by sail, they were at the mercy of winds and currents, so their paths were erratic and their journey was silent. There were reports of sea serpents all the time then. But once the noisy steam engine was invented and ships began sticking to specific shipping routes, reports significantly dropped. The sea monsters got smart and learned to avoid those shipping lanes, which left more ocean open for cryptids to hang out in."

"We think your dad saw some cryptids," Stephanie

chimed in. "He claimed never to have seen one, but sometimes he'd come back to us a bit more energized and with a secret smile on his face, as if he knew something nobody else did."

Clivo knew that smile, too. Russell hadn't had it after every "dig" he went on, but every so often he'd come home and spend the next few days quietly laughing and talking to himself. When Clivo's mom had been alive, he'd sometimes heard the two of them giggling and whispering to each other late at night. Those must have been the times when his dad had found a cryptid.

"So, what's Nessie's origin story?" Clivo asked.

"Hah! Wouldn't you like to know!" Adam retorted. He held up a plastic-bound booklet with a cover that read:

THE LOCH NESS MONSTER
ORIGIN STORY

BY ADAM LOWITZKI

(with minor help from Charles,
Amelia, Stephanie, and Hernando)

"We compiled this for your old man. He was going to buy it, but it seems he kicked the bucket before he had the—"

Amelia elbowed him in the ribs.

"Ow! What?"

"So, I guess I should buy it instead. If that's okay with you guys," Clivo said.

Adam narrowed his eyes and picked up a banana from a bowl in an area stocked with snacks and drinks, then took his sweet time peeling it as he sized up Clivo.

"Well, it won't be cheap . . ."

"I can give you five thousand dollars," Clivo offered, hoping it was enough.

Adam choked on his bite of fruit.

"We accept! We accept!" Charles yelled, tripping on a table in his haste to get to Clivo.

Amelia and Stephanie encircled Clivo. Amelia spoke first.

"Clivo, you don't have to pay us that much. Your dad didn't. I mean, I'd love to quit my job at the bookstore, don't get me wrong, but we can't take that."

"I'm fine with quitting my job at the Cryptid Collection," Charles said, bouncing up and down with excitement. "That place is lame and their intel on the Yeti is totally weak."

"Seriously, at the end of the day, this is all for fun," Stephanie agreed. "It's not like we *actually* helped your dad find a cryptid. Now, *that* would be worth five thousand dollars."

Clivo pulled out his wallet again and handed Adam, who was still choking on his banana, a wad of bills.

"Trust me, you guys are worth it," Clivo assured them. "Oh, any chance you could give me a receipt?"

A short time later, Clivo exited the basement by the outdoor stairs, the crypto-research manual stuffed in his backpack and a ticket booked online for a midnight red-eye flight direct to London, where he would catch a connecting flight to Inverness.

The door creaked below him and he turned to find Stephanie tentatively poking her head out.

"Hey, you okay? You seem a bit overwhelmed with everything," she asked as she climbed up to stand beside him. She really was like a gentle, inquisitive mouse, Clivo thought.

Clivo looked at the ground bashfully. "Is it that obvious?"

Stephanie smiled. "Not really. But I've done some reading on analyzing facial expressions. You're exhibiting at least three facial tics that signify overwhelming stress."

Clivo groaned. "Great, you can hack satellites *and* read minds?"

"Not minds, just faces," Stephanie said with a grin. "But I'm sure with enough practice I could develop my telekinetic abilities."

Clivo stuck his hands in his pockets. "It's just, I'm pretty new to this whole world. I mean, like twenty-four-hours new, so it's a lot to wrap my head around."

"Don't worry, you'll get used to it. And I'm sure your dad would be proud of you for continuing to do . . . whatever it was he did."

Clivo thought about that. He lowered his voice and spoke to her quietly. "Actually, I'm not so sure about that. I mean, did my dad even mention me to you guys? To be honest, he never told me about any of this, and I'm trying to figure out why."

Stephanie paused for a moment, then spoke slowly, as though sensing she was treading on delicate ground.

"Your dad never told us anything about his personal life. But I can tell you that he always seemed to be in a rush. Like he wanted our information so he could quickly do what he needed to do and return home. It's funny, sometimes I felt like he didn't really need us, that he'd be able to figure the stuff out on his own, and had done so in the past. We just made things easier for him, because he had more important things to get home for."

Clivo forced a smile. It'd be nice if that had been true.

"Thanks." He turned to go. "I'll let you know how my search for Nessie goes."

"We'll look forward to that." Stephanie placed her hand on Clivo's arm. "Clivo, I'm sure your dad had his reasons for things. You may not understand them, and they may not make sense, but I'm sure he was just doing what he thought was best for you."

"And you know this because you knew my father better than I did?" Clivo hung his head, shocked by the bitterness in his voice. "I'm sorry, I didn't mean that. I know you're just trying to help."

Stephanie smiled again and wrapped her arms around herself. A slight wind blew, cartwheeling yellow leaves down the stairs, where they gathered in a corner. "I know this because I know parents. None of them have a clue about what they're doing, and most of them flat-out stink at it. But at the end of the day, they're just trying to do their best."

"You kinda sound like an eighty-year-old wisewoman," Clivo joked, though her words did make him feel somewhat better.

Stephanie wrinkled up her face. "I do, don't I? It's horrible. Maybe I should learn some good jokes or something, just to lighten up my conversational skills a bit."

They stood for a moment in awkward silence until Charles came to the rescue by sticking his head out the door.

"Are you guys making out? Gawd! Get a room or something!"

"And that's my exit cue," Stephanie said, all the blood in her body apparently rushing to her cheeks. "Oh, here's my phone number. You know, just in case Nessie's giving you some trouble. And my e-mail and Skype info. You can contact me through smoke signals, too; I'm good at reading those. Just kidding, I'm not. Okay, that was a dumb joke. I'm going to go now."

Stephanie scurried down the stairs as Clivo looked at her number in disbelief. A smile crept onto his face as he realized that, for the first time in a while, he had made some new friends.

Wednesday

XII

Clivo had until Monday night to get back home before Pearl did, so going to Scotland to find Nessie seemed like the right thing to do while he had the time.

Adam had ordered a cab to take Clivo back to the airport, and at check-in he was assigned another Serge-like muscular chaperone who escorted him through the terminal. Unlike Serge, this bodyguard didn't say a word and had an unnerving habit of cracking his knuckles every time some wayward fellow traveler glanced their way.

It was Clivo's first time flying over the ocean, at least that he could remember, but his palatial first-class seat tempered any nervousness he felt. It was like his own little pod, complete with a seat that converted into a flat bed and another personal TV with even more options than on his previous flight.

Some of the first-class patrons eyed him with suspicion, probably thinking he was a bratty spoiled kid who was going to wreak havoc. Others stared a little too hard, as if trying to place him, perhaps wondering if he was some famous boy-band member. How else could a kid be flying alone across the ocean in first class?

The attention made Clivo uncomfortable. His checked backpack was carrying a tranquilizer gun, after all. He reminded himself to keep his head down and remain as inconspicuous as possible. The last thing he needed was to make a ruckus and draw focus to himself.

After a delicious dinner of filet mignon and scalloped potatoes, Clivo lay down and fell into a deep sleep, only to be interrupted by a loud noise piercing his dream.

"Sir? Sir! I need you to shut your phone off."

A woman was talking in his ear and someone was shaking him. Clivo snorted awake to find a flight attendant standing over him, looking like she was about to throw him out the door without a parachute. A deafening sound like an incoming-torpedo warning filled the cabin.

"What's going on?" Clivo asked, wiping a bit of drool from his lip. He looked frantically around, only to find the other passengers staring daggers at him.

"Your phone, sir. Off. Now."

Clivo patted his pockets and pulled out his satellite phone, which was the source of the alarm. It had never rung before, so Clivo had had no idea that Douglas had programmed it loud enough to wake the dead, though it was hardly surprising.

"Sorry, this is a new phone, I don't really know how to . . ." Clivo couldn't find a button to shut the darn thing off, and now people in coach were standing up to see what was going on.

"Phones are not allowed in-flight, sir. Phones aren't even supposed to work at thirty-five thousand feet, so—"

"I'm sorry, it's a satellite phone, so I guess, well—I guess it does work this high . . ." Clivo said with a forced chuckle, still frantically fumbling with the machine.

"Sir, if you insist on being a disturbance—"

"No, no, I'm not disturbing. I'll just answer it and hang up."

Clivo pressed the screen and the piercing sound stopped, only to be replaced by Douglas's roaring voice on speaker-phone.

"Galldarnit, kid! What the—"

"Mr. Chancery! Hi!" Clivo pressed the screen again, but there still were no options that would turn off the phone.

"I told you to fly coach! Since when is first class considered coach? In what stupid, self-involved universe has first class all of a sudden become coach?" Douglas's voice reverberated throughout the aircraft.

Clivo spoke in a whisper. "Mr. Chancery, if you could keep your voice down, I'm currently on an airplane . . ."

"I know you're on an airplane! And I know you're not in coach! I don't pay you to fly first class, I pay you to fly

COACH! After this you'll be lucky if I let you sit in the cargo hold with the pets."

Clivo heard a few people behind him gasp.

"I understand, and next time I will fly coach. Now, will you please hang up before they throw me out over the ocean?"

"Keep your mouth open on the way down, kid, your head needs a refill of air."

The phone thankfully shut off and Clivo quickly stuck it under his seat in case Douglas called back.

"I'm sorry, that won't happen again. Unless he finds something else to yell at me for, which he probably will."

Clivo sheepishly looked at the flight attendant, who was desperately trying not to laugh.

"And I thought I had to deal with jerks," she said with a wink.

You don't know the half of it, Clivo thought.

After a nerve-racking hour or so when Clivo jumped at every ding and beep, he eventually passed out and slept until the plane landed in London. He grabbed his backpack from baggage claim and headed to Customs, which was housed in a sterile white-tiled room filled with hordes of people waiting to be allowed into the country.

Clivo joined a long line and watched nervously as passengers presented their passports to stern-faced men and women who asked a myriad of questions. One male passenger had his suitcase rifled through by two guards in crisp collared shirts who pulled something out of the bag and waved it in front of his face. The man loudly protested and was promptly carried away, kicking and screaming, into a corner room where the heavy door slammed shut, cutting off his wails. Clivo's bag, holding the tranquilizer gun, suddenly felt very heavy in his hand.

Just as it was Clivo's turn to be questioned, a tall man wearing a dapper suit with a monocle squeezed over one eye came rushing up.

"Mr. Wren? My apologies, I was delayed by another Diamond Cardholder who refused to let their pet tiger go through the metal detector at Security. Follow me, please." The bodyguard, who spoke with a proper British accent, ushered Clivo quickly through Customs.

This escort was tall and lithe and not muscular like the other ones had been, but something about his fluid movements made Clivo feel like the man could handle himself just fine in case of attack. Walking through the bustling terminal, Clivo was amazed by the different languages being spoken by the travelers, who came from all over the world. He felt a tinge of excitement when he was able to understand several of the dialects that reached his ear.

Clivo finally boarded his connecting flight, and after a bumpy ride in a small puddle jumper he arrived in Inverness, Scotland. His escort there was a muscular man with red freckles who was wearing a kilt, and Clivo was pretty sure the guy had a dagger strapped to his thigh. Fortunately, the man didn't have to stab anybody as they walked through the airport, but he did remind Clivo to change his dollars to the local currency of pounds.

Since Douglas had yelled at him for flying first class, he figured that renting a nice car and driver was out of the question. So he hopped in a cab and asked the driver to take him to a place he could stay at that was as close as possible to Loch Ness, which ended up being the small village of Drumnadrochit, a forty-minute drive away. The taxi was a black, boxy thing, like something out of a spy film. The cabbie, who had an extremely large double chin, was silent during their ride, which Clivo didn't mind. After the long journey he was happy to have a few quiet moments to himself.

The cabbie dropped him off at a quaint inn called Nessie's Hideaway, as announced on a faded wooden sign that dangled from a rusty metal chain. Clivo handed the man his fare and added a tip on top, which was a good one judging by the man's nod in thanks, his double chin bouncing up and down in appreciation.

The lobby of the inn looked like someone's cozy living room, with dark-green carpet and little tables covered with doilies. Pictures and figurines of Nessie coated every available space, and the air smelled like spicy tea. Clivo rang a bell on a desk and a tiny old woman came through a side door. She was maybe five feet tall, with ruddy cheeks and curly hair dyed a shockingly bright shade of red.

"Ta, laddie! What can I help ya with?"

"Hi, I'm looking for a room." Clivo gave the woman a big smile, hoping she wouldn't start pestering him with questions about where his parents were. Maybe the fact that he towered over the innkeeper would help.

Thankfully the woman's face perked up with excitement. "Ah, you've come ta look fer Nessay, have ya?"

"Uh—"

"Don't be embarrassed about it. You're never too old to believe in monstahs." She introduced herself as Mrs. McRory and took care of the paperwork quickly. To Clivo's surprise, she didn't seem overly impressed with the Diamond Card. "Now, come along," she said, shuffling toward the stairs. "Let's get ya settled."

Mrs. McRory led him to his room on the second floor and left him alone, but not before giving him the inn's wi-fi password and a list of good pubs to go to for dinner.

"Whatever ya do, avoid the Loch Ness Lickster, they serve the cheapest cuts of mutton, tha crooks."

She shut the door behind her, and Clivo put his backpack down and examined the room. It was small and whimsical, with rose-patterned wallpaper and a polished chest of drawers. The bed was large, with a fluffy down comforter that smelled of lavender. Clivo resisted the urge to lie down and fall asleep for the night. It was barely four o'clock in the afternoon, but he felt like he had been up all night. This must be what jet lag felt like.

He pulled out his laptop to e-mail Jerry, figuring his friend would be wondering where he was by now.

Subject: Major Math Problem

Hey Coops—

Sorry to be out of touch, my phone is extinct. I'm far away, searching for a solution to that math problem.

I may not be back for Friday dinner, so please make up an excuse for your parents. I'll be in touch soon.

Wren

Clivo sent the e-mail before he could second-guess what he had written. It felt weird writing everything in code, like there was somebody watching over his shoulder, but he figured, better safe than sorry. And Jerry would understand everything, anyway. Sometimes they talked better in code.

Then he sent an e-mail to Aunt Pearl telling her he'd dropped his phone in the sink, so if she called he wouldn't pick up, but he swore that he hadn't stolen anything or lit the house on fire.

He put the laptop to the side and picked up the small metal case Douglas had given him. He unlatched the case and opened it, revealing heavy foam padding with several objects neatly tucked into it, including the tranquilizer darts and gun. The first thing he pulled out must have been the blood sampler. It was a small, hard-plastic cylinder with a digital readout at one end and a retractable needle at the other. A dial with the words SKIN, SCALE, BLUBBER etched on it was probably used to determine how powerfully the needle needed to be projected. He turned the dial to SKIN but couldn't figure out how the darn thing worked. He spun the contraption around and the needle end brushed against his leg. He instantly heard a click, which was followed by a rather painful stab in his thigh.

"Ow, son of a bat," Clivo swore, rubbing his leg.

The digital reader came to life, the words BLOOD CAPTURED blinking on the screen. He watched a drop of his blood travel up a glass vial into the cylinder. Once it reached the top, there was a quick beep and the words NOT IMMORTAL blinked on the screen.

"Good to know," Clivo muttered.

Finally, he pulled out the crypto-research manual,

propped his back up on some pillows, and settled in to read, practically hearing Adam's voice doing the narration:

Loch Ness Monster History

The Loch Ness Monster, or Nessie, as some knucklehead named her (I'd prefer something more foreboding, like Lochenstein), was originally documented in the first few hundred years A.D. The tribes that roamed the Scottish Highlands back then, collectively called the Picts, carved animals on the standing stones they erected. All the animals were recognizable, save one—wait for it—a large, dinosaur-like creature with a long neck and flippers. Thus the legend of a strange creature living in the loch was born and, two thousand years later, people are still enthralled with the poorly named beast.

The earliest written reference to Nessie (Amelia says I can't call her Lochenstein or I totally would) is from a biography of Saint Columba, who, in the sixth century A.D., was in Scotland trying to convert the Picts to Christianity. Apparently the holy roller needed to cross Loch Ness, so he ordered one of his followers, Lugne Mocumin, to swim across and fetch a boat. Well, Lugne had just begun swimming when Nessie surfaced and lunged at the poor guy, her jaws open and ready for her snack. But Columba raised his hands and said something all medieval, like, "Hark! Don't ye attack!" and the beast didn't.

Modern interest in Lochenessie (What? It's close enough!) began in 1933, when a road completed along the shore allowed clear views of the loch. A couple out for a drive saw a large animal cross the road in front of them. When they reported it to the local paper, the reporter called the creature "The Loch Ness Monster," and thus the name was born.

Since then, thousands of people have taken photos and videos of what they think is Nessie, but most of the photos have been determined to be hoaxes or don't show anything substantial enough to be considered proof. Still, over four thousand eyewitness reports have been recorded. Some are obvious hoaxes from nutters; others are pretty cool accounts from regular people.

Searches

Nessie is, by far, the most searched-for cryptid in the world. All in all, she's been the subject of at least eight major expeditions using underwater photography and sonar. Each search yielded at least one unexplained sonar hit. Still, there is nothing concrete enough to warrant a definite claim of having found the creature. Thus, the mystery of Nessie lives on.

My Origin Story Theory (with a teeny-tiny bit of help from some other people already mentioned)

Okay, here we go: the good stuff. Most people think Nessie is either an old plesiosaur dinosaur or (according to someone clearly off their rocker) an alien dropped off from the mother ship. The alien theory doesn't work because, well, it's just cheesy. But what if, what if—and go with me here on this—what if Nessiestein is a plesiosaur that never went extinct? *How, Adam? How could that be?* you ask. Well, now listen. The loch was formed ten thousand years ago, at what just happened to be the end of an ice age. Isn't it possible that a plesiosaur was trapped, alive, in ice sixty-five million years ago and once the ice melted, it was revived, happy as could be in Scotland? A total shock for the creature, seeing as how plesiosaurs are known to have lived in the warmer climate of Australia and it would totally suck to wake up in the dreary hills of Scotland with no coconuts anywhere to be found. But not impossible—after all, plesiosaur fossils have been found as far north as England, so Nessie wouldn't have had to travel that far on the ice-train express. But still, how would such a thing be possible? Well, we have evidence of humans being revived hours after drowning in a freezing lake because the cold basically put their bodies on pause. Cryonics is a whole science we've barely skimmed the surface of. It's a bit far-fetched that something could still live after being frozen for sixty-five million years, but we don't have any proof that it's totally impossible. After all, what do we really know about a dinosaur's physiology? We know that they ate and roared a lot and had humongous bones; beyond that, it's anyone's guess what their bodies were really like.

Now, the next question: How is it that she's now been alive for ten thousand years? Answer: She's not alive, she's slowly dying. After living sixty-five million years, her body basically forgot how to die, or the process has been majorly slowed down, but she will die. Her body just has to remember how.

How Nessielochenstein Hides

This one is a bit unclear, but yours truly does have some theories. First of all, sonar sometimes sees Nessie, sometimes not. That's easy: the floor of Loch Ness is filled with eighty feet of soft sediment. All she has to do is bury herself within the muck, much like a stingray does, and she will avoid detection. Next: visual sightings of Nessie drastically dropped off after the late 1980s. Did she die? Did she swim to the ocean through one of the many rivers? Nope. Let me offer you an alternative explanation: Chernobyl.

After the nuclear reactor in the Ukraine melted down in 1986, the wind carried a layer of radioactive material to the loch. Do you know what a dose of radioactivity can do to something? Now, I'm not saying—but I might be saying—that I've heard tales of super-secret experiments done on (unwilling) volunteers with high doses of radiation. Weird crap happens, man. One of the side effects is what it does to the skin. What if, what if Nessie, because of all her digging in the sedi-ment to avoid detection, developed an ability, through the radiation, to puff out her blubbery skin. That would accen-tuate her goose bumps, for lack of a bet-ter term. Since her massive body is mainly made of water, her skin bumps would fill with water, thus creating a reflective illusion. In essence, she would be invis-ible by mirroring her surroundings. Far-fetched, but you come up with a better idea, Wren.

Clivo paused for a moment, wondering when Adam had had the time to personalize this document for him. Then he realized it had been meant for his dad; Nessie was going to be his next catch. His chest tightened with the wish that his dad were still around, that he was the one sitting here instead of him. But his dad was gone and it was now up to him to find the immortal cryptid. The enormity of what he was doing settled on him, and things suddenly felt horribly real. He could practically hear Douglas yelling at him not to mess it up.

Extra Proof

Now, in case you think this is all a bunch of malarkey, it may very well be. A hypothesis is just a theory until proven, and the only concrete proof is to have Nessie in your hot little hands. However, beyond my nifty little idea, we also have some data that back up our intelligent deductions. Stephanie was able to hack into the National Science Foundation's computer system, and we found something very interesting. Now, normally our government doesn't get involved in cryptid research (waste of money, they say—don't get me started) but sometimes they do (on the down-low of course).

In the 1970s an organized series of searches for Nessie took place. We're talking the works: underwater strobe-lit cameras, full sonar canvassing, radar instruments up the wazoo. And this wasn't a crazy group of yahoos, either. No sir, these were bona fide scientists from Concord, New Hampshire's Academy of Applied Science, including a bunch of smart MIT folks. After trolling the loch for days on end they never found Nessie, but they did uncover some unexplained stuff. Most of it we know about—inexplicable large hits on the sonar, a fuzzy picture of what looks like a flipper, bizarre underwater noises. But they also found something else that was never released to the public because scientists like to hog all the good stuff for themselves. Several different water samples were taken around the loch and analyzed. Nothing of interest showed up except in one little beaker. Upon close examination, cells were discovered whose DNA we've never seen before. It might be dinosaur DNA, the first complete sample ever discovered. The phenomenal thing is that the cells were living. They found living cells chockfull of dinosaur DNA! They must be Nessie's cells, sloughed off her skin or something.

The MIT researchers handed the find
over to the NSF, and now who knows what the
NSF is doing with the sample. Hopefully
they're trying to clone the cells to bring
back the dinosaurs, 'cause that'd be sweet.

Clivo closed the packet and rubbed his eyes, amazed
by what he had just read. Was it possible that Nessie was
an ancient, thawed-out, radioactive dinosaur?

With any luck, he'd soon find out.

Clivo grabbed his backpack with the gun and blood sampler and headed down to the loch. He was dragging with
exhaustion from his travels, but was too nervous to even
consider getting any rest. He pocketed the keys Mrs. McRory
had given him and made sure to lock the front door to the
inn as he exited, seeing as how the sun was going down
and night would be falling fast.

Clivo was glad he had put on a heavier sweatshirt as
the cool humid air sent a chill through his bones. It was a
good half-hour walk to the loch through rolling green hills
on a windy two-lane road where cars sped past him at
breakneck speed.

He rounded a bend and was finally greeted by the
magnificent sight of the loch spreading out before him. It
was narrow enough that he could see the other side, but so

long he couldn't see either end. The water was a deep gray, reflecting the mist that hovered just above its surface. Along the shore, various campfires were lit, their flames dancing like tiny torches.

Clivo slid down a gravelly hill and stumbled across an old man sitting next to a bonfire, a rickety van parked off to the side. He turned his head as Clivo appeared. The man's face was lined with wrinkles, and a scraggly beard reached to his chest.

"Oh, sorry, sir, I didn't mean to disturb you," Clivo said, turning to go.

"It's the best time to look for her, don't you think?" the man said, gesturing toward the loch.

"Um, I don't know, it's my first time, actually," Clivo said, stopping to talk.

The man's eyes sparkled. "I remember my first time. I was here on vacation and something about the mystery of the loch just got to me. I tried to go back home and forget about this place and my fruitless vigil, but I couldn't. It draws me back every year."

Clivo looked at the loch again, where more campfires were springing up on the distant shore. "Are all those fires surrounded by people looking for Nessie, too?"

"Sure are," the man said, stirring the fire with a stick. "This place tends to draw people who are looking for a bit of danger and magic in a world seen as being completely over-explored."

"Have you ever seen her?" Clivo asked hopefully.

The man winked at him. "Sometimes I think I've seen a glimpse of her. Not much, but enough to keep me believing."

"And how long have you been coming here, sir?"

The man cackled. "Twenty-five years. And I've loved every day of it."

Clivo's heart sank. Twenty-five years? Clivo had until Sunday to find Nessie. If Aunt Pearl returned home to find him missing, she'd have the entire army sent after him.

"I guess I'll wander around a bit, then, see if she's around tonight," Clivo said.

"Here," the man said, handing Clivo a roasted sausage in a bun. "Best to keep your energy up."

Clivo took the food, realizing how hungry he was. "Thank you, sir. Good luck."

"You as well, fellow explorer, you as well."

Clivo wandered down the bank, the task in front of him seeming impossible. How was he supposed to find something that couldn't be seen? That lived in water, no less? If all the fires were evidence of the number of people who were looking for Nessie but had never found her, how would he be any different?

He finally found a secluded spot on the shore, propped his tranquilizer gun on his lap, and waited.

The stars began to twinkle and the moon glinted on the water. He thought about his dad, about how he had found cryptids. Twelve of them. How had he done it? The Myth Blasters had helped him research which ones existed, but not how to find them. His dad had done that part, and he had been training Clivo to do the same.

His mind flipped through the training—how to fight, how to camp, how to travel over rough terrain. But those were all survival skills. How had his dad been training him to *find* the mysterious beasts?

He'd been taught how to observe things, how to track, how to see little things that were just slightly out of place. But how would that help him see something invisible?

A thought struck Clivo: he had to summon the creature. He couldn't go to Nessie; Nessie had to come to him.

Clivo stood on the bank and began making whatever sounds he thought Nessie would recognize. He yelled, he bleated, he cooed like he had heard Jerry do to his dog. He patted the water and made noise until his throat was dry and his voice was scratchy.

But nothing came to shore. No head peeked above the surface, no curious eyes peered from the black water.

Clivo traveled up and down the shore of the loch, steering clear of the fires where people were gathered, everyone silently looking for the mystery that lay beneath the waves.

After hours of calling, when it must have been well past midnight, he sat down in exhaustion. Howls from up and down the shore pierced through the night air. His calls must have spurred the other searchers to do the same, but he doubted that wolf howls would draw Nessie to shore.

He hung his head and sifted through his memories for any nugget his father might have taught him. A vision of them sitting around the campfire on one of their mountain excursions popped up—his dad preparing a hearty meal to warm their bellies after a day spent in the snow.

"How's your dinner, C?" his father asked as they enjoyed roasted beans and potatoes.

"It's great, Russell, thanks," Clivo said as he wolfed down the meal. His dad had just returned after having been gone for over a month, and it was almost like they were getting to know each another again.

Russell stared off into the distance, his eyes sad and his spoon forgotten in his bowl. It seemed like he wanted to say something—something important—but he shook his head and simply said, "Just remember, C, everything needs to eat. Food is the one thing that brings everybody to the table."

Clivo's head snapped up. Food. Nessie needed to eat. Obviously she had been eating in the loch for the past ten thousand years, but what did she eat before that, when she was a dinosaur? Maybe she missed the food she had eaten sixty-five million years ago.

Clivo quickly picked up his things and dragged his tired body back to the inn. The road was empty of cars at this late hour, and all was silent save for the baaing sheep wandering in the fields. The tiny village was quiet as well, with all the windows shuttered for the night and the only light coming from the twinkling stars.

Clivo quietly unlocked the front door to the inn and crept to his room, wincing at every creaky step. He flipped open his computer and did a quick search for what plesiosaurs ate, a triumphant smile coming to his lips.

He collapsed onto the downy fluff of his pillow, thinking about where he could find the treats in the village. As his mind was racing through the possibilities, he fell into a deep, jet-lagged sleep.

Thursday

XIII

The following morning Clivo shuddered awake to a gentle knocking on his door. He opened his eyes and for a moment had no idea where he was. He crawled out of bed and opened the door to find a smiling Mrs. McRory wearing a red dress even brighter than her hair.

"Oh, good! Y'er alive! I thought perhaps the cold Scottish weather had finished ya off."

"No, Mrs. McRory, I guess I'm just not used to jet lag," Clivo said with a yawn, shocked that it was already morning.

"Well, if you'd like I can bring in a tray of breakfast if ya need a few more minutes of shut-eye. Otherwise y'er welcome ta come down and meet the other guests. Just a nice couple from Amsterdam and a fellow monstah seeker like yourself from Luxembourg."

Clivo stopped midstretch. Luxembourg? Hadn't Douglas said something about there being a cryptid catcher from Luxembourg? It could just be a coincidence, or the guy could have followed him here.

"When did the guy from Luxembourg check in, Mrs. McRory?"

"Oh, last night, shortly after you. I told him there was an American monstah seeker here as well and he seemed very excited by that. I put him in the room right next to ya," she said, pointing to the wall opposite Clivo's bed.

Clivo swallowed. Douglas had said the catchers from Luxembourg were idiots, but that didn't mean much coming from Douglas. Douglas thought everyone was an idiot. What Douglas hadn't mentioned was if they were dangerous or not. They were going after something that promised immortality, after all. People would probably put up quite a fight for that. For the first time, Clivo wondered if his dad had taught him jujitsu so he could protect himself from dangerous cryptids, or from dangerous people.

Clivo considered making a run for it. There was probably a back door he could slip out of and . . . what? Run away? Give up on the hunt? He considered it, strongly. But running before he was even in official danger didn't seem to be the bravest choice. Smartest, yes. Bravest, no. If the Luxembourger attacked him, however, *then* he could reconsider things. Douglas could hardly expect him to put his life at risk battling other catchers.

"I'll come down for breakfast, Mrs. McRory. I'd love to meet the other guests." If he wasn't going to make a run for it, he at least wanted to see what the other catcher looked like, just in case the guy tried to follow him.

"I figgered ya was a nice laddie," she said, standing on tiptoe to affectionately sweep the hair out of his eyes. "Now, put on some clean knickers and come on down, then. I've made some fresh blood puddin' for yer fry-up."

Clivo's stomach growled, though from nerves or hunger he couldn't quite tell.

Clivo walked hesitantly into the dining room, his eyes quickly scanning the other three guests. The couple from Amsterdam seemed eager to talk to anybody except each other, and the guy from Luxembourg looked like something out of an old spy movie. He must have been in his midtwenties, with dark hair slicked back to within an inch of its life and a pencil-thin mustache (that could have been drawn on), and wore a black-and-white-striped shirt and a red ascot tied neatly around his neck. And he was very petite—even Mrs. McRory could easily have taken him in a fight.

"Ah, here ya are!" the innkeeper said, putting down a steaming plate of fried eggs, grilled tomatoes, bacon, toast, and two things that looked like burned pancakes, which must have been slices of blood pudding. "Folks, this is Clivo Wren. Clivo, this is Mr. and Mrs. De Vries."

"Charmed to meet you!" Mrs. De Vries said, giving Clivo a smile that caused her plump cheeks to swallow her eyes. She had a thick accent and an even thicker body, and her face flushed red in odd, splotchy places.

Mr. De Vries simply sat with his hands resting on his round belly and didn't say a word. By the sour look on his chubby face, Clivo got the feeling coming to Loch Ness had hardly been his idea.

"And this is Blirgenbach Schnauss," Mrs. McRory continued, making a sound like she was clearing her throat while pronouncing his name. "He's here to find Nessay, too, so maybe you boys can look togethah."

"I look forward to that," Blirgenbach said seriously, his big black eyes never leaving Clivo's face. Clivo swallowed and took a seat at the table.

Mrs. McRory bustled in and out of the kitchen, leaving the guests to fend for themselves with the conversation. The food was delicious, and Clivo even took a nibble of the blood pudding. Weird, but not as bad as he'd expected.

"So you two really think you can find her?" Mrs. De Vries asked, piling her plate with fresh toast.

Clivo and Blirgenbach looked at each other, each waiting for the other to speak. Clivo cleared his throat. "I mean, that'd be really exciting. But at the end of the day she's just a legend, right?"

Blirgenbach kept his inappropriately wide-eyed stare trained on Clivo. "Of course. Just a legend. Like the chupacabra, Honey Island Swamp Monster, and blue tiger."

Clivo snapped his head up so fast he almost gave himself whiplash. Those were the last three cryptids his father had caught. A slow smile spread across Blirgenbach's face.

"Game on," Blirgenbach said, chomping a mouthful of blood pudding.

Clivo instantly lost his appetite. This guy was definitely a competing cryptid catcher. But was he dangerous? Blirgenbach's small size didn't make him look it, but Clivo had learned through jujitsu that you didn't need to be big to pack a solid punch.

"Well, I happen to believe in legends," Mrs. De Vries began, shaking Clivo out of his thoughts.

"Here we go," Mr. De Vries muttered.

"A few years ago, a flock of fairies flew into my bedroom and blessed me with the gift of psychic vision." Mrs. De Vries was smiling so hard it looked like her splotchy cheeks were going to burst.

"And what have you seen?" Clivo asked, trying to avoid Blirgenbach's stabbing stare. If Clivo hadn't known any better, he'd have sworn the guy was trying to hypnotize him with his eyeballs.

"A whole lotta nothin'," Mr. De Vries murmured.

"I can read people's auras. I can sense the magical energy of a place. I can tell when evil is lurking," Mrs. De Vries countered.

"Is evil lurking here?" Clivo asked quickly.

Mrs. De Vries put down her fork. "I don't know, I haven't opened myself up to communicating with the imps here yet. Let me try."

Mr. De Vries made a snoring sound and pretended to fall asleep with his chin on his chest. Mrs. De Vries ignored him, closed her eyes, and opened her palms to the ceiling. She slowed her breathing and began humming quietly. After a moment she opened her eyes and gazed calmly about the room.

A smile pulled at her lips but suddenly stopped before it lifted her bubbly cheeks. Her eyes flicked to Blirgenbach and her face dropped. Her mouth opened slightly and she looked at Clivo with concern, her flushed red face going ghostly white.

"Oh," she said quietly.

"What is it?" Clivo asked, dropping his fork onto his plate.

Mrs. De Vries pulled on her husband's sleeve. "Come on, honey. We forgot we have someplace to be in a few minutes."

"We don't have anyplace to be! Let me enjoy my breakfast, you pestering ninny."

Mrs. De Vries whispered something in her husband's ear. "Is that right?" he muttered, glancing at Blirgenbach. Without another word, the two of them grabbed their plates (and a few extra slices of buttered toast) and quickly retreated to their room.

"Let the games begin," Blirgenbach said, wiping his mouth with a napkin.

Clivo got up from the table with such haste that he knocked over his chair and juice glass. As he sprinted up the stairs to his room, Blirgenbach was right behind him.

Clivo ran into his room and slammed the door in Blirgenbach's face. Now he regretted his decision not to just sneak out the back and run away. The Luxembourger was bent on finding Nessie, and something about his small body oozed big danger. Clivo shuddered with the realization that he was now officially in peril.

He threw on a sweatshirt and grabbed all of his equipment, stuffing it into his backpack. He looked out the peephole of his door and saw Blirgenbach hiding awkwardly behind a banister, waiting for him to exit. Clivo went to his window and checked out the drop, groaning when he saw there was nothing but air between him and the flower patch two stories below. He quickly tore off the bedsheets, tied them together, and anchored them to the bedpost. He'd seen this done in the movies, so hopefully it worked in real life, too. But come to think of it, it never worked that well in the movies, either.

He grabbed the sheets and lowered his body out the window to test the makeshift rope. Miraculously, the sheets held. He glanced at the Luxembourger's window to see if he was watching him with his creepy stare, but the curtains were drawn tight. Clivo was shimmying his way down the side of the inn, feeling pretty proud of himself, when he heard a ripping sound.

"Oh, shoot!"

The sheets tore loose and Clivo fell backward to what he figured was certain death. But just as he began to fall, his back hit the ground, the blow worsened by the metal case in his backpack.

"Oh." Clivo looked around, realizing he must have been just a few inches from the ground when the sheet gave way.

He scrambled up and ran toward the village. He'd have to come up with some good excuse to give sweet Mrs. McRory for why her nice sheets were ripped and hanging out the window. But for now he had to focus on racing a threatening Luxembourger to the Loch Ness Monster.

After a good five minutes of running toward town with constant panicked backward glances to make sure he wasn't being followed, Clivo slowed his pace and began looking for the seafood restaurant he had noticed on the list of pubs Mrs. McRory had given him. He needed to buy the treats to summon Nessie with before heading to the loch. Fortunately, the village was small, so it took him just a few streets to find a wooden building with a sign painted on the window: SULLY'S SEAFOOD PALACE.

Clivo pulled on the front door, but it was locked. He stomped his foot in frustration. It was just a matter of time before the Luxembourger realized he was gone and came after him. He needed to move quickly.

Clivo heard some banging from the cobblestone alley next to the building and discovered a bald man with the longest earlobes he'd ever seen unloading crates from a truck. By the smell of them, the crates were definitely filled with some kind of seafood.

"Excuse me, sir, do you have any clams or snails in there?" Clivo asked quickly, looking down the street to make sure Blirgenbach wasn't creeping up on him.

The man quit his unloading and eyed the boy. "Maybe, maybe not. What's it to ya?"

Clivo pulled out a wad of bills. "Can I buy all of your clams and snails, please? It's really important."

The man sniffed. "I only deliver what's been ordered. If ya haven't ordered, ya don't get a delivery."

"But I really need them, and I can give you a lot of money!" Clivo said, waving the bills again.

The man grabbed a crate from the van. "And ruin this restaurant's day by not delivering their order? Not a chance. Now bugger off!"

The man entered a side door to drop off the crate, leaving Clivo with only one option: thievery.

"Pearl would be so upset with me for doing this," Clivo mumbled to himself.

He slammed the door shut behind the man and wedged a metal trash can under the knob, locking him inside.

"Hey! I said no delivery unless you order!" the man roared, banging on the door.

"And I politely asked you to reconsider!" Clivo said, climbing into the back of the van.

He frantically looked through the boxes and crates. Most were filled with ice-covered dead fish of all shapes and sizes, and one held a bunch of live lobsters that reached for him with their pincers. He finally opened a box and saw a gorgeous sight—a pile of smooth white clams, one of the foods that plesiosaurs had eaten millions of years before, when they'd lived in the oceans.

"I hope you like these, Nessie," Clivo said, hoisting the box and gathering himself to climb out of the van.

Just as he turned, a sight greeted him that made his belly sink. Standing at the front of the alley was the deliveryman, who was staring at him with anger and menace. Clivo had completely forgotten about the exit through the front door of the restaurant.

"Come here, ye dafty bampot!"

Clivo dropped the box of clams and grabbed a crate of small fish, tipping it over so the slippery bodies covered the narrow alley in front of him. He grabbed the clams and ran the opposite way as fast as he could just as he heard the swish, thump, and swearing of the man falling on his backside.

As Clivo ran away, he dropped a wad of cash by the van. "I'm sorry about the fish!"

He peeled out of the alley and stopped dead in his tracks as Blirgenbach came running around the other corner, his ridiculous mustache twitching with excitement.

"Gotcha!" Blirgenbach yelled.

Clivo reversed direction and ran into the street, jumping on the hood of the first car that drove by. The elderly male driver, who was wearing a beret with a bushy pompom on top, looked at Clivo in surprise, his long, wiry eyebrows just about jumping off his face. He slammed on the brakes and Clivo went flying onto the street, the box of clams clutched to his chest. He stumbled to his feet and jumped in the passenger seat, much to the surprise of the man sitting next to him.

Clivo slammed the door locks down. "I'm sorry, this is an emergency, can you please take me to Loch Ness?"

"But I'm not going toward Loch Ness," the man said as slowly as sap running down a tree.

"Please, I'll pay you a hundred pounds." Clivo was breathing so heavily he thought his lungs were going to explode.

The old man scratched his head. "With the price of petrol, that may hardly be worth goin' out of me way fer."

Blirgenbach ran up and began slamming his palms on the windshield. The old man didn't seem to notice and just kept rambling on.

"Although a hundred pounds could fetch me a nice meal at the pub."

"I tried to be reasonable, Clivo!" Blirgenbach yelled, coming around to the passenger's side window.

Clivo ducked his head, reached down, and pushed his hand against the old man's shoe, revving the gas and causing the car to squeal forward.

"Mercy!"

The old man gripped the steering wheel and struggled to keep the car on the road as it roared out of the village.

"Two hundred pounds! But you have to go fast!" Clivo bellowed from the floor of the car, where he was still pressing on the accelerator.

"I'll take it, I'll take it!"

Clivo sat up in his seat and the car slowed down. The old man turned to him and instead of a look of terror, he had an expression of pure glee on his face.

"Did ya say fast?" He slammed his foot against the accelerator and the car lurched forward, throwing Clivo back into his seat. "Didn't know ya got into the car of a former rally car driver, now did ya? Fasten yer seat belt, laddie, we're going for a ride!"

The car sped forward even faster and the man swerved around cars in front of them, narrowly avoiding oncoming traffic on the two-lane road. Clivo scrambled to get his seat belt on and was both relieved and terrified that he had chosen such a fast getaway car. He looked behind him, figuring it would have been impossible for Blirgenbach to follow him, unless the Luxembourger had lucked out and happened upon a retired race car driver, too.

"First time in Scotland?" the man shouted over the roar of the engine.

"Huh? Oh, yes. First time out of America—since I was a baby, anyway," Clivo replied, clutching the clams to his chest in sheer terror as they narrowly avoided an oncoming tour bus.

"Just a lovely time of year to be here. Name's Ainsley."

"Clivo."

"Weird name. Anyway, if you look over there, Clivo, ya can see a little wooden shed. Me mother was born there at night right in the middle of a wicked hailstorm. Her papa wanted to name her Stormy, but Nana would na hear of it!"

Ainsley laughed and looked at Clivo just as a hay truck was coming at them.

"Hay!" Clivo managed to shout.

Ainsley veered back into their lane and kept his tour-guide spiel going.

"Now, I'm gonna let ya in on a wee secret. Over there are some standin' magic stones discovered when I was a young man. People come from all over tha world to see what the fairy people created. But—and this stays between us—it was actually me and my pal Johnny who did that one drunken night with the help of a donkey and a bottle of whiskey!"

Ainsley laughed so hard his foot pressed even more heavily on the gas pedal.

After the longest and scariest five minutes of Clivo's life, Ainsley squealed the car to a halt in front of the large ruins of a castle. URQUHART CASTLE, a sign read.

"Thank you so much. If you got me here any faster, we would have been in warp speed." Clivo handed Ainsley two hundred pounds, trying to hide the shaking of his hand.

"Ah, keep it, lad. I haven't had that much fun in years. The missus won't let me drive above the speed limit, so this adventure put a bit of sass back in the old stallion."

Ainsley peeled the car away with a wave out the window, shooting pebbles and dust in Clivo's face.

Clivo spit a piece of gravel from his mouth and quickly took cover behind a bush to make sure he hadn't been followed. A few cars passed by, but he didn't see Blirgenbach's hypnotizing eyes peering from any of the windows.

He scurried past the crumbling stones of the castle and

found a secluded spot on the rocky shore. Putting down the box of clams that was now dripping with slimy, pungent juice, he tossed a few as far as he could into the water. The loch was so massive it would have taken a ton of clams to spread them throughout the entire thing, but this was all he had—one box, and not a whole lot of time.

Clivo emptied almost all the clams into the loch and waited in the most comfortable spot he could find, his eyes scanning the water, searching for any movement that was out of the ordinary.

And he waited.

And waited.

And then he fell asleep.

Foiled again by jet lag.

He had no idea how long he'd been zonked out or what had awakened him.

His heart was pounding at a frantic pace, and he stood up and walked to the edge of the water, hoping with every fiber of his being. He tried to ignore the feeling that he could spend the next twenty-five years waiting for the mysterious creature to appear. But his dad had found cryptids, so it must be possible. It was the possibility, no matter how remote, that gave Clivo hope.

What happened next hit him like a tree branch.

Actually, it was a tree branch, whacking against the side of his head with a sickening cracking sound. He saw stars and really hoped the sound of breaking had been from the branch, not his skull.

He whirled around just as the branch was pulled underneath his chin and pressed painfully against his throat.

"Where is she?" Blirgenbach hissed in his ear. For such a small guy, his strength was astounding.

"As if I have any idea," Clivo gagged, grabbing the stick with both hands. He could barely breathe.

"What's in the box?"

Blirgenbach jerked the branch tighter and Clivo gasped.

"None of your business."

Clivo was scared, but he forced himself to remember that he had been in this position hundreds of times in jujitsu class. It was an easy move to get out of; he just had to calm his nerves so his muscles could relax and respond to what he told them to do. He took what breath he could and closed his eyes, thankfully feeling his seized muscles releasing just a little, but it was enough.

"I'd appreciate it," Clivo began, his voice coming out in a wheeze, "if you'd give me some *space*."

Clivo flipped his body forward, throwing Blirgenbach over his shoulder in a somersault.

Blirgenbach quickly sprang up into a crouch, ready for battle. Clivo did the same, though his pose was rather different. The Luxembourger seemed a bit surprised.

"Hmmm, tae kwon do?" Clivo asked, forcing his trembling voice to sound calm.

Blirgenbach nodded. "And you? Kung fu?"

"Jujitsu."

Blirgenbach snorted. "Your father trained you terribly." He kept his distance and warmed up with a series of movements, exhaling in sharp bursts as he kicked and punched his way through a routine that was obviously meant to intimidate. Clivo tensed in preparation for the fight.

Finally Blirgenbach sprang. He came at Clivo like a Tasmanian devil trapped in a hurricane, a force of energy ready to obliterate. When Blirgenbach was almost upon him, Clivo nipped to the side and simply pushed Blirgenbach from behind, encouraging him to go even faster in the direction he was headed. Blirgenbach flew forward, his body thrown off-balance by the sudden absence of a victim in front of him, and ran face-first into a tree. He let out a groan and fell backward, stiff as a plank and out cold.

Clivo put his hands on his thighs and took some deep breaths. His heart was pumping so quickly that his vision darkened from all the blood rushing through his head. He thought he was going to pass out, but after a few moments the adrenaline left his body and his vision returned. He rubbed his throat, definitely feeling a bruise coming on. He had never been in a life-or-death situation before, and it was an experience he could definitely do without.

He only had minutes before Blirgenbach would awake. He grabbed the remaining clams and waded as far into the cold water as he could stand. He held the food in his hands, bringing it forward like a sacred offering.

"Come on, girl. Come get your snack."

He kept his arms out, silently calling with all of his being for Nessie to appear. His arms began to ache, but still he waited, hoping for the impossible to happen.

Just as his arms began to slip to his sides, a movement churned the water in front of him. At first it was just a few bubbles; then the surface of the water stirred and rose up, rolling off some dark, glistening mass.

Clivo's breathing stopped as Nessie surfaced before him. She was black as a seal, with a lumpy body the length of a bus and a neck as long as a giraffe's. She looked right at him with large, blinking eyes that sat on a comically small head. Her wide mouth was chewing the clams and she let out a purring noise like a happy cat.

Clivo was so surprised he just stood there, amazed by the beautiful creature in front of him.

Then his body sprang back to life as he suddenly re-membered his task.

He ran to his backpack and grabbed the tranquilizer

gun, fitting it with the largest dart available. He knelt down and took Nessie in his sights.

His finger hesitated on the trigger. Shooting such an amazing being seemed wrong, but he reminded himself that it would just put her to sleep, and if some evil person like Blirgenbach found her, her fate would be much worse.

"I'm really sorry, but I have to do this," he whispered.

He fired.

A roar of surprise and distress pierced his ears and Nessie collapsed in the shallows.

Clivo ran into the loch with the blood sampler, not caring about the sting of the cold water against his body. He wrapped his arms around Nessie's neck, and with a grunt of exertion he set the dial to BLUBBER and pressed the device to her body.

A click sounded and the screen glowed to life. Clivo crawled to shore and waited anxiously as a drop of bright red blood traveled up the tube. After what felt like forever, the screen finally flashed its message: NOT IMMORTAL.

Clivo exhaled and collapsed to the ground, all the energy leaving his body. As disappointed as he was that she was not the immortal cryptid, he was also relieved. He couldn't handle any more excitement in one day.

He turned to look at Nessie, with her head near the water's edge and the waves gently lapping against her shiny skin.

"Hey, girl, don't worry, you'll wake up soon," Clivo said,

stepping into the water again and reaching out to stroke the creature's cold head, which was long and flat like an iron.

Nessie's eyes opened just a sliver and the beast glanced at Clivo. Her long neck shuddered and she raised her head. The orbs of her eyes were like black marbles, reflecting the shimmering of the sun. She let out a weak bleat and regarded Clivo with curiosity.

"It's okay, I won't let anything happen to you. I promise," Clivo said.

He pulled out his satellite phone and snapped a picture of her to send to Douglas. Then Clivo snapped a selfie with the drowsy monster behind him to show to Jerry later.

A flash of light caught Clivo's eye, followed by another and another. He looked up at Urquhart Castle, where tourists were snapping photos from the crumbling ramparts. Picture after picture and video after video were being taken of him and Nessie, and there was no way he could stop it.

His body seized in a panic. Nessie was a majestic creature who deserved to be left alone. What would happen if people got ahold of her? They would throw her in a zoo! Clivo looked at the peaceful being and sprang into action. As people began to run from the castle to get a closer look, Clivo started hooting and waving his arms, startling Nessie, who sleepily retreated farther into the water. He splashed after her, shouting with all his might, ignoring the frigid water that wrapped around his limbs. As soon as they were far enough out that Nessie was floating on her own, her body shimmered and disappeared. Clivo waded back to shore, saying goodbye to a being he hoped nobody would ever see again.

Friday

XIV

Roughly twenty-four hours later, Clivo was getting a lecture.

"The Loch Ness Monster is currently on the cover of every single newspaper in the world. One of the most mysterious legendary creatures ever to grace our imaginations is now making bigger headlines than the moon landing did."

Douglas's voice was miraculously calm. Clivo kept expecting the old man to yell or throw stuff or at the very least to hit him with his cane. Instead the old man slowly wandered around the den in Clivo's house, poking his stick at the books on the shelves while quietly musing to himself.

"Thousands of years the creature has lived. Undisturbed, unmolested, free to float around its giant bathtub in naïve bliss. Then you send one stupid kid in there to do a simple job and the whole thing goes to Hades."

"Mr. Chancery—" Clivo began.

"Mouth closed!" Douglas interrupted, pointing his

cane in Clivo's face. "You may not speak. You have lost the privilege of speaking."

Clivo grunted and sat back in his chair. Douglas continued walking around the room, shaking his head and muttering to himself. The roaring of the furnace reverberated through the brass vents and Clivo was grateful for the blast of hot air, even though it sounded like a ghost rattling its chains. After the chill of Scotland it felt like he was never going to be warm again, so he had cranked up the heat even though it was warm outside.

"It's fairly simple. Find legendary creatures without letting the rest of the world in on the secret. Straightforward. Easy. Your dad didn't have a problem with it. But you. YOU!"

Clivo flinched as Douglas threw a newspaper at his feet. It featured a photo of Nessie taken right before Clivo had tranquilized her. Fortunately, the photo was from far enough away that Clivo's face was a blur, and the paper didn't mention his name. The headline simply read LOCH NESS MONSTER NO MATCH FOR MYSTERIOUS TEENAGER. Clivo's heart sank with the realization that he had blown the lid off a legend thousands of years old.

"You call that being secretive?" Douglas bellowed. Finally he was raising his voice. That made Clivo more comfortable. It was the silent, deadly Douglas that made him nervous. "Well? Speak!"

"Mr. Chancery, I did the best I could! Considering

that creepy catcher from Luxembourg was trying to kill me, it's a miracle I made it out of there alive! How Blirgenbach found me, by the way, is a total mystery."

Douglas heaved his body down into the chair next to Clivo. "Bah, I told him where to find you."

Now it was Clivo's voice that turned deathly quiet. "You did what?"

"Had to see what you were made of. Had to make sure you didn't turn yellow at the first sign of trouble. If you couldn't handle the Luxembourger I would have lost all faith in you. The guy's harmless."

Clivo couldn't believe his ears. "Harmless? He's a master in tae kwon do!"

"And you're a master in jujitsu. Hardly a fair matchup, wouldn't you say?"

Clivo wasn't sure how to take the compliment. "He hit me in the head with a tree branch!"

"And you ran his face into a tree trunk. Sounds like someone's being a sore winner."

Clivo gave up. Obviously he wasn't going to get any sympathy from Douglas. Heck, Douglas had *sent* Blirgenbach to attack him.

Clivo rubbed his eyes, wishing he could erase the last twenty-four hours from his mind. After making sure Nessie had safely vanished before the throng of tourists from the castle arrived, he'd done the only thing he could think of. He'd gathered his stuff and *run*.

He'd left nothing behind at the inn, so he simply hitched a ride to Inverness, where he caught a cab to the airport and booked a flight through London back to the States. Nine hours in coach on his flight over the ocean made him never want to fly again, especially sandwiched between two heavyset, hairy men who both seemed averse to wearing deodorant.

Once the taxi from the Denver airport had driven up the dirt driveway to his house, he'd thought he could finally get some rest—until a knock at the door as soon as he had put his backpack down ruined that idea. He'd known he was going to hear from Douglas; he just hadn't been expecting a personal visit.

"Well, since I passed your test, can you please promise me no more surprises?" Clivo begged, running his hands through his greasy hair. He was in desperate need of a shower. "Making it through the day without tranquilizing myself is hard enough; I don't need martial arts masters from every country coming after me, as well."

"Oh, I'm sorry, are you under the assumption that I still need your services?" Douglas asked a little too innocently.

That made Clivo freeze. "Well, yeah. I mean, I know I messed up a little bit with Nessie—"

"A little bit?" Douglas looked at him in disbelief.

"Okay—a lot. But I found her, Mr. Chancery. I *did* find her. You have to give me some credit for that. Now we know she's not the immortal. And what about the contract? Don't you *have* to work with me?"

Douglas casually polished the top of his cane with a handkerchief he'd pulled from his pocket. "I agreed to work with you because your father promised you'd be good. If you're not, the contract is null and void, and I'm free to find someone who's actually competent. I think at this point even your father would tell me to go hire someone else."

Clivo stared out the window, Douglas's words stinging him. Maybe if his dad hadn't lied to him his whole life, he'd be better at this.

"Well," Douglas began, pushing himself to his feet, "if you think you can actually do your job without screwing it up this time, I'll give you another shot. But only because your father was the best and I'd like to believe his gene pool didn't totally dry up with you."

Clivo stood up as well. "Thank you, Mr. Chancery. I won't let you down this time."

Douglas eyed him head to toe. "See that you don't. The name of Wren has great prestige in the cryptid-catching world. The greatest. Don't let it go to waste on you."

Douglas turned his back and hobbled toward the front door.

"My dad believed I could do this, Mr. Chancery. I know he did." Clivo didn't know why he yelled that at

Douglas's back; maybe he just needed to hear himself say it.

Douglas stopped, but he didn't bother turning around. "Did he tell you that?"

"No, not exactly. But—"

"Yeah, he never said that to me, either."

Douglas slammed the front door, leaving Clivo standing alone in the dark house.

Clivo wanted to take a scalding-hot bath and go to bed, but it was only early evening. If he went to bed now, he'd probably wake up at three A.M., and the last thing he wanted was to wander around the deserted house in the middle of the night. Part of him longed for Aunt Pearl to come home, just to hear the squeaking of her rocking chair as she did her nightly reading. Even having a clinging cat around to pet didn't sound so bad. One cat.

He turned on as many lights as he could to rid the house of shadows and grabbed a soda, hoping the sugar would keep him awake a bit longer. He wanted to talk to Jerry, but he figured his friend would still be at work. Clivo settled for e-mailing him, just to let him know that he was okay.

After a good, hot shower, Clivo sat in the living room, which was eerily quiet, save for the occasional rattling of the basement furnace. His mind was jumbled with fatigue, jet lag, and the miserable awareness that his first catch had been a disaster. Clivo wished that Bernie, the coat of armor, would come to life just so he had someone to talk to.

After a long hour of feeling like the walls were closing in on him, he realized he hadn't touched base with the Myth Blasters. He riffled through his wallet, which was still soaked from the loch, and pulled out Stephanie's Skype address. It was getting late two time zones away, but they were all probably eager for the inside scoop.

He opened his computer and the screen shortly lit up with Stephanie's face, the other Myth Blasters ecstatically crowding behind her.

"Dude! Took you long enough!" Charles exclaimed. "We've been dying to know what happened in Scotland!"

Adam elbowed his way in front of the camera. "She could turn invisible with her radioactive skin, couldn't she?"

"She went invisible all right," Clivo confirmed, the excited energy of the group perking up his spirits a bit.

Adam pumped his fists in triumph. "I'm so smart, it's actually painful." He disappeared from view.

"So, I guess the Nessie news is everywhere?" Clivo asked.

"You could say that," Amelia said, excitedly joining the conversation. "It's all over the internet, and the crypto chat rooms have totally exploded."

"It's big, man. Really big," Charles chimed in. "This is the first confirmation of a cryptid in, like, forever, man! As soon as you vouch for us we're gonna be total celebrities now! When is the 'mysterious teen' going to come forward?"

Adam ran back to the camera and shoved Charles out of the way. "We're already thinking about quitting school and turning this into a business. For a hefty fee we'll send people a package that contains info on where to find the creature of their choice. It'll be a whole new level of adventure tourism."

"And we're hoping to be on the cover of *Scientific Secrets* magazine," Charles said, pushing Adam out of the way. "We're thinking, like, a military-style cover, with us looking totally Rambo, standing on a tank or something. We're going to have fangirls everywhere!"

"Whoa, you guys," Clivo said, holding his hands up. "I'm staying out of the spotlight. We can't let anybody know that other cryptids actually exist!"

"What are you talking about, dude?" Charles snorted. "That's the whole point of doing this, right? To prove that cryptozoology isn't a pseudo-science, but an important branch of *actual* science? I mean, *man*, we found something the scientific community brushed off as being a fabricated legend. And we can find more. This is the beginning, man. You just opened up a realm where legends are real, and trust me, we *will* be at the forefront of that exploration. It's our dream come true."

"Yeah, we want to be known as *the* crypto experts," Adam added. "Even just so McConaughey's clan can bow down to our dominance."

"And that's exactly what you *can't* do," Clivo said, trying to keep his panic at bay. "The whole point of what I do is to find these creatures in secret. Most of the world considers them legends, and it needs to stay that way."

Stephanie spoke up. She seemed to be the only Blaster not totally carried away by their potential new celebrity. "Why, Clivo? Why go through all the trouble of finding something only to keep that information to yourself? It doesn't make sense."

"Yeah, dude, you're going to have to give us some pretty good reasons why this strapping body shouldn't be on the cover of every magazine," Adam said, motioning to his skeletal frame.

Clivo rubbed his hands over his face. Now he understood why his father had never told the Myth Blasters about the creatures he caught—he'd known they'd spill the secret the first chance they got. "You guys, I can't tell you the exact reasons. All I can tell you is that it is *extremely* important that nobody knows more cryptids exist. And nobody, I mean *nobody*, can know that you guys helped me. If word gets out about this, it could put you in a lot of danger."

The last sentence seemed to subdue the group a bit. They looked at each other with concern and Charles glanced at his chest, as if expecting a gun laser to be pointed there.

Stephanie was the first one to speak. "What kind of danger?"

Clivo grimaced at the fear in her voice, and at the thought of Blirgenbach storming the basement to attack them. If the boys tried to use their bush-league karate moves on the Luxembourger, a few measly safe words wouldn't help them. And according to Douglas, Blirgenbach was the *least* dangerous of the other cryptid catchers. Clivo hated that he had inadvertently put his new friends at risk.

"All I know is that there are some other people out there who do what I do, and none of them are nice. If they discover you can find cryptids, they'll come after you."

"But, if that happens we'll just give them the information," Amelia said. "I mean, if people are going to storm in here all mean-like, we'll give them what they want and send them on their way."

"And if you do that," Clivo pointed out, "you could be putting humankind at risk."

"Putting humankind at risk?" Stephanie asked, her voice quiet. "Aren't you being a little dramatic?"

Clivo shook his head adamantly. "I'm not. I promise. I can't tell you more than that."

Adam grabbed Stephanie's computer and held it up to

his face. "Okay, listen, buddy. In just a few minutes you dash our dreams of international stardom while saying the fate of the world is in our hands and, oh yeah, our lives are also in danger. Sorry, pal, this calls for full disclosure."

"Full," Charles said, turning the computer to his face, his buck teeth taking up half the screen.

"Full," Hernando quietly agreed, pulling the computer to him. "Please."

"I can't do it, you guys," Clivo persisted. "That's not my call to make."

Stephanie took her computer back. "So whose call *is* it?"

Clivo realized he didn't have an answer for that. Did he need Douglas's permission to tell them? He didn't think his dad had told Douglas about the Myth Blasters, so maybe he shouldn't, either. Besides, he didn't want to subject them to the nasty man. But his dad also hadn't told the Myth Blasters about the immortal cryptid. Russell had kept everything a secret, and that had allowed Russell Wren to become the best cryptid catcher out there. Clivo had to make sure he did the same, even just for the reason of keeping them safe.

"What exactly did my dad say about what he did?"

Charles stuck his head in the frame. "We told you, dude. That he was an archaeologist who was curious about the local folklore when he went on digs."

"And he told you he never found anything, right?"

Amelia piped in. "Well, yes, but like we said he sometimes acted—"

"And that's all you know about me," Clivo interrupted. "I'm a junior archaeologist who travels the world on digs and you guys teach me about the local lore. That's it. That's all we are. Okay?"

The Myth Blasters all looked at one another. Stephanie hit the mute button so Clivo couldn't hear what they were saying, but it was obviously a heated discussion, with Adam making big swooping motions with his arms. He looked like a convulsing flamingo. Finally, Charles undid the mute button.

"Sorry, dude. No."

"What do you mean, no?" Clivo asked, dropping his head into his hands.

"First of all, there's no such thing as a junior archaeologist, so that whole cover story is totally weak. Second, that's all we knew about your *dad*. You can't come in here and adopt what was clearly just his cover story and expect that we'll trust you the same."

Stephanie tucked a stray hair behind her ear and smiled. "Remember, Clivo, your dad was doing things the way that *he* thought was best. You need to make your own decisions. *You* need to decide if keeping us in the dark is really the way you want to handle this."

Amelia tilted the computer toward her. "If things really

have gotten as bad as you say they have, don't you think it'd be better to have a few more people on your side?"

"But you guys are on my side, aren't you?" Clivo asked, getting worried. His days as a cryptid catcher would come to an abrupt end without their help.

"We *were* on your side," Amelia said, casually picking at a hangnail. "Until you put us in danger. Now, we may have to reconsider."

"Guys—" Clivo began.

"The game has changed, Clivo," Stephanie said, bringing the computer close to her so it was like they were the only ones talking. A candle must have been burning close by, because she had a golden glow bouncing off her blue eyes. "You got us involved. Way involved. It may have been an accident, but that's where we stand. You're the captain of this ship, and you get to make the rules now. We might be willing to jump on board with you all the way; we just need to know what trip we're buying a ticket for."

Clivo exhaled. "Obviously you haven't been working on your jokes, because you still sound like a wise old sage."

"Oh, actually I have! Knock knock."

"Fine. Who's there?"

"Harry."

"Harry who?"

"Harry up, it's cold out here!" Stephanie laughed. "But I'm serious, Clivo. We can be a team; you just need to tell us everything. We can't help you fight something if we don't know what it is."

Clivo leaned back in his chair. Stephanie was right. He knew she was. He couldn't just ask them to keep everything they knew a secret without telling them why. They had a right to know what he had gotten them into, even just so they could protect themselves better. Besides, he didn't like being a cryptid catcher all alone. Having people he could talk to besides cantankerous Douglas, who sent assassins after him, wouldn't be so bad. But how could he trust them to keep the immortal cryptid a secret? He figured that that's how trust goes—you give it to someone and then hope like crazy they don't throw it away.

Clivo took a deep breath. "Okay. Here goes. My dad was a cryptid catcher. His job was to find legendary creatures, photograph them, and let them go. Thanks to your research he found the Honey Island Swamp Monster, a blue tiger, and a chupacabra. All in all, he found twelve cryptids before the chupacabra killed him. My job is to keep looking for the one special cryptid that's different from all of the others."

The gang all dropped their mouths in disbelief.

Hernando swooned and fainted onto the floor.

Stephanie was the first one to recover. "I'm so sorry about your dad. You told us he died, but not how. That's horrible."

"Thank you," Clivo said, mustering a wan smile.

Charles got up close to the camera. "Did he find the Yeti?"

"Not now, Charles!" Amelia said, waving him away.

"I wanna know if he found the Yeti!" Charles whined.

Stephanie blinked, as if trying to sort through her thoughts. "Okay, so your dad found other cryptids. I think it needs to be stated that that's—"

"FRICKIN' AMAZING!" Adam yelled from the back of the room, where he was once again shadowboxing.

"I'd use the word 'phenomenal.' But why didn't he tell us any of this?" Stephanie pressed.

"For the same reason I couldn't tell you," Clivo replied.

"And that reason would be what?"

Clivo looked at Amelia, who was furiously chewing her lip. "Amelia, any chance you have the lost prophecies of Nostradamus on your bookshelf?"

"The lost prophecies of Nostradamus? Sure, who doesn't? Give me a second, will you?"

"All creatures, one blood. Some remain hidden, others come fore. In one who is hidden, the blood is gone, replaced by the spring of life. A silver lightning drop of eternity."

Amelia quit reading and looked up at the camera on her screen.

Apparently she had gotten over her initial shock that more cryptids had been found and had clicked into her scientific-thinking brain. So had the rest of the Blasters, who had sat and listened intently to the prophecy. Even Hernando had recovered from his faint, though the fall had caused him to hit his head on the arm of a desk chair, giving him a welt on his forehead, which he was currently icing with a can of Moxie soda.

"Okay, so you believe in the immortal cryptid interpretation of this prophecy," Amelia said.

"You know that interpretation, too?" Clivo asked.

"We're the Myth Blasters. We know everything."

"What else do you know about these prophecies?"

Amelia spun her nose ring around between her thumb and a finger. "Nostradamus was a French apothecary and seer from the sixteenth century. He looked at astrology and determined future events based on how the stars were lined up during past events. A lot of his prophecies came true."

"And what else do you know about this particular prophecy?" Clivo asked, relieved to finally have someone to talk to about all this. Already he was feeling better about letting the Myth Blasters in on everything, the way he wished his father had with him.

Amelia furrowed her brow. "That's the funny thing. Most people regarded this prophecy as talking about Jesus, so it was discounted as not being a prophecy so much as a poem about history. How Jesus rose from the grave to become immortal. But that doesn't really fit. Nostradamus didn't write poems, he wrote predictions. So obviously everyone has been reading this wrong—everyone except us, of course."

Clivo leaned in closer. "So, according to this prophecy, do you believe the immortal cryptid exists?"

Amelia closed the book. "The Myth Blasters don't *believe* anything. We prove stuff. As far as the immortal cryptid being a possibility? *Anything* is possible. All you have to do is prove it. It's a shame your dad didn't let us know that he was looking for the immortal. We wasted a lot of time not researching which cryptid it might be."

"But you understand why he had to keep this a secret, right?" Clivo said.

Adam popped his head in. "What? Keep the power of immortality a secret so it doesn't fall into the wrong hands? Dude, that's pretty self-explanatory."

"Right. So, does that mean you guys are interested in still helping me?" Clivo pressed. "If you want to be on the covers of magazines and stuff, I guess I can't stop you. You'll be famous and probably rich. But I won't be able to work with you anymore, and you'll be dooming every cryptid out there to being discovered and thrown into captivity, or worse. We need to be a team that works under the radar, on the fringe, kept hidden from those who are also searching for the elixir of life. Like spies who live in the daylight but operate from the shadows. No one can know what you do, or what you know. It could be dangerous, and there will be people trolling for you, hunting you, wanting your information. Your sole mission will be to keep secrets, no matter what the cost."

Clivo looked at the Blasters with anticipation, hoping that his speech had worked. It was maybe a touch overdramatic, but he figured these guys would dig that kind of thing. He was also hoping they wouldn't be mad at him for involving them in something so dangerous.

"When you put it like that it sounds kinda awesome," Charles finally said.

Stephanie once again pressed the mute button. The Blasters engaged in another heated conversation, Adam gesticulating wildly and going so far as to lift up his shirt and point at his concave chest. He was probably bemoaning his lost magazine covers.

Stephanie finally turned the sound back on. "Okay, we're in. What do you need from us first?"

Relief swept over Clivo. "Thanks, guys. And I'm sorry I put you in danger, I really had no idea. So, I guess this means that we're officially a team?"

Adam waved his finger back and forth. "Just to be clear, you're part of *our* team. And 'danger' is my middle name. Continue."

Clivo held his hands up in apology. "Absolutely, *your* team." He rubbed his forehead and thought about their next step. "So, I guess that while you try to narrow down who the immortal cryptid might be, I need another one to catch."

"You got it, captain," Stephanie said.

"Oh, you might want to start looking for the immortal wherever Russian, Arabic, Japanese, and Hindustani are spoken," Clivo offered.

Amelia looked puzzled. "Why?"

"My mom and dad taught me those languages. If they thought I'd become a catcher, I can't imagine they chose those randomly. They were probably narrowing the search for me."

"Okay, I'll need to record you speaking those languages," Amelia said. "The specific dialect they taught you could give us a smaller search region. Speaking of which, we only helped your dad find three cryptids. How did he find the other nine?"

"That's a good question," Clivo said, realizing he hadn't considered that. "Maybe others helped him. I didn't know about you guys, so it's possible there were other helpers like you out there. Or maybe he was just good enough to figure it out alone."

Amelia furrowed her brow. "I don't like the idea that there are others like us out there who can find cryptids. Guys, keep your radar up for any groups that seem to know more than they should."

"Oh, and if you guys wouldn't mind finding me a cryptid closer to home and in a warm climate, I'd appreciate it.

I've had enough of cold and airplanes for a while," Clivo added.

"No problem, dude, we're almost done compiling our Yeti info," Charles said, rubbing his hands together excitedly.

"I said a warm climate!" Clivo protested.

"Yeah, yeah," Charles said before clicking a button, causing the screen to go blank.

XV

Clivo signed off and leaned back in his chair in relief.
He had messed up his first catch, but he was now part of a
brilliant team that was hot on the trail of the immortal. For
the first time since this whole adventure had begun, a bit
of confidence was slowly creeping into his bones.

That confidence quickly scurried away when he realized that he had no idea how he was going to keep doing this
without telling Aunt Pearl, not to mention how he could skip
school. He couldn't just drop out; there'd be no reasonable
excuse to give for that. And there were only so many salsa-
dancing competitions he could send Pearl to. Finding the
next cryptid was all of a sudden the least of his worries.

He was jerked out of his thoughts by a sharp knock on
his door. Clivo groaned. What did Douglas want now?

He dragged himself to the front door like a guy headed
to the firing squad and peeked through the window. But it
wasn't Douglas. Standing on the porch were two people, a
girl about Clivo's age and a man who looked to be in his
midtwenties. The girl was dressed in a skirt and light

sweater, while the guy wore a lab coat with a scarf around his neck. Clivo didn't recognize them, but was relieved they weren't Douglas. However, his relief lasted for less than a second when he wondered if they were sent by Douglas to attack him.

He was about to sneak away from the window when the man saw him.

"Mr. Wren! Mr. Wren! Can we have a moment of your time? It's excruciatingly important!" he said in a proper British accent.

The man's dark hair was disheveled and he wore a pair of thick-rimmed glasses. He was very small, with a tiny head, and was carrying an official-looking black briefcase, which was handcuffed to his thin wrist. There was something familiar about him, though Clivo couldn't place exactly what.

"Who are you?" Clivo asked suspiciously through the glass.

"As if we're going to shout that out here where every spy could hear us, Mr. Wren! If you could please just let us in—"

"Did Douglas send you? If so you can tell him—"

"Who in bloody heck is Douglas? Look, I'm Thomas J. Forthwit the Third and behind me is Lana Hampton," the man said.

"Oh. What do you want?"

"For the love of Buddha and his belly, that's what we want to tell you! If you could just let us in—" Thomas's voice was nearing hysteria.

Lana stepped forward and spoke, her voice calm and also distinctly British. She had auburn hair pulled up in a sleek bun and seemed like a nerdy intellectual save for the vampire-red lipstick that stood out on her pale face. What sort of parents let a girl walk around with that kind of makeup? Obviously, British ones.

"Mr. Wren, we're from the International Secret Order of Mythological Beasts, Legends, and Cryptid Catchers, and we'd like to speak with you regarding—"

Thomas stepped in front of Lana and continued his tirade. "Something that can only be spoken about *inside*!"

Lana leaned toward Thomas and attempted to calm him down.

"Thomas, we agreed that we would approach Mr. Wren *nicely*, in a way that wouldn't frighten him," she said in a hushed voice.

"I am asking nicely!" Thomas yelled, almost dropping the briefcase. "I'm asking as nicely as I can, considering that humanity is about to be doomed to extinction!"

"That's great. That's not frightening at all." Lana sighed. She looked at Clivo and gave him a reassuring smile.

Thomas took a deep breath and shook his head as if he was cracking his neck.

"Mr. Wren, might it be possible for us to enter your abode to speak with you *calmly* about how we need your help *immediately* to stop the destruction of life as we know it?"

"Much better," Lana said, giving Thomas a condescending pat on the shoulder.

Clivo's palms got sweaty. Now what was going on? If Douglas hadn't sent these people, Clivo knew he should probably defuse whatever problem there was before the cranky old man got a whiff of it.

He opened the door and Thomas plowed inside, not waiting for an invitation.

"That's better. Now, it should be in southeast Alaska, but it's not. It just disappeared!" Thomas slammed the briefcase on the dining room table, the handcuffs' chain clanking on the wood.

"Thomas, I think we should probably start from the beginning," Lana said as she calmly stepped inside. She looked at Clivo with an incredibly penetrating stare, as if she were trying to read his mind.

"Fine, start from the beginning, and while you chit-chat I'll try not to hear the doomsday clock ticking in my head," Thomas moaned.

Lana clasped her hands in front of her. "Mr. Wren, we're here because you found Nessie, yes?"

"The Loch Ness Monster?" Clivo scoffed. "No, that wasn't me."

"Then why were you checked in at Nessie's Hideaway the same day she was found and why are you wearing the same sweatshirt as the kid in all the pictures who found her?" Thomas yelled, shaking a newspaper in Clivo's face.

Lana took the paper away from Thomas. "What Thomas means to say is . . . congratulations. You're officially a cryptid catcher."

Clivo pursed his lips. He was still totally thrown off-balance about who these people were, how they knew it was he who had caught Nessie, and what they wanted.

Thomas snorted. "Although you did make Nessie front-page news. No offense, but your skills at going undetected pretty much stink."

Clivo glared at Thomas but didn't say anything.

"Anyway," Lana said, shooting Thomas a glance, "due to the success of finding your first catch, we'd like to welcome you to the International Secret Order of Mythological Beasts, Legends, and Cryptid Catchers."

"Or ISOMBLCC for short," Thomas agreed.

"Although we just call it the Order," Lana added.

Clivo stared at the weird pair in front of him. "Not that I know a lot about the cryptid-catching world, but I've never heard of you guys."

Thomas scoffed. "That's why it's a *secret* order, chief. Our information is so classified that I have to wear this briefcase chained to my wrist." He rattled the handcuffs dramatically.

"Is that supposed to make you look official?" Clivo asked with a raised eyebrow.

"The *lab coat* makes me look official, the handcuffs just make me look cool."

Clivo rolled his eyes.

"Moving on," Lana continued, clearing her throat, "we're here because we want you to join us. The search for cryptids is an extremely crucial endeavor. I'm sure you understand why."

Clivo wondered if she was referring to the immortal, but he didn't say anything for fear he'd be revealing something she didn't know. There was something about Lana and Thomas that made Clivo's hair stand on end, as if he shouldn't completely trust them.

"Moons of Jupiter, just say it!" Thomas interrupted. "The immortal! The ultimate! The elixir of eternal life!"

Clivo shifted his feet uncertainly. "You guys know about the immortal?"

"No, we traveled all the way from England to this bizarre little house hidden on a mountain to talk about fairies!" Thomas yelled.

Clivo gritted his teeth and glared at Thomas. Did everyone in the cryptid-catching world have to yell at him all the time?

Lana put a calming hand on Thomas's shoulder. "Again, what Thomas is *trying* to say, is that, yes, we know about the immortal. But what *you* may not understand is how fraught with peril the search for it is."

"What do you mean?" Clivo asked.

Lana's voice got quieter and her long eyelashes cast shadows that looked like spiders' legs down her cheeks. "There's an evil resistance gathering whose only goal is to find the immortal and take over the world. And they're getting stronger."

Clivo thought about his mom shaking the old Egyptian rattle to protect him from the God of Storms and wondered if she'd known about this gathering storm of evil.

"I'm listening," Clivo said.

Lana's voice picked up speed. "There are many people searching for the immortal, and most of them want to use it for their own villainous purposes. There's only a handful of us who want to use its power for good, but we're sorely outnumbered. We've decided the only way to find the immortal before the nefarious ones do is to band together and help one another. That's why the Order was created many years ago."

"And how did you become a part of it?" Clivo asked, his brow furrowing. "You're a little young to join something like this, aren't you?"

"Says the world's youngest catcher," Lana said with a slight smile. "Thomas and I are cousins and our family has searched for the immortal for generations. When you come from a long line of catchers, going to school and studying arithmetic seems a little unimportant, wouldn't you agree?"

Clivo was still eyeing Thomas and Lana warily. "And how do you know I'm one of the good guys? How do you know I'm a catcher at all?"

"Because you're Russell Wren's son," Thomas said. "He's *legendary* in the legend world. And as far as we know, he's the only person to have actually caught a cryptid. Unless you're some kind of rebelling brat, we're pretty sure you're following in his footsteps."

"Speaking of which, is that his study?" Lana asked, gazing eagerly toward Russell's den.

Clivo nodded but quickly added, "But there's nothing in there. Nothing that would tell you how he caught cryptids."

"Still, may I? Like Thomas said, he's a legend. It'd be an honor to see where he worked," Lana persisted.

Clivo figured that letting Lana and Thomas take a peek in the den couldn't hurt. There was nothing in there—nothing that he hadn't gone through a hundred times already. "A quick look, just don't touch anything."

Lana and Thomas tore into the den like hungry wolves would a steak. They frantically scanned the room, as if searching for some clue. Thomas reached out to take a book, but Clivo grabbed his wrist firmly. "I said no touching."

"Ow! Message received, tough guy!" Thomas said, rubbing his wrist.

Lana and Thomas continued wandering around the room, desperately searching for something that Clivo already knew wasn't there.

"It's amazing in here," Lana finally said, "like standing in the room of a genius."

"I like the smell in here, too," Thomas agreed. "It smells like success."

Clivo leaned against a bookshelf and crossed his arms. He was wary of Lana and Thomas, but curious whether they could reveal something about why his dad had kept it all a secret from him. "So, um, did you know my dad? Was he part of the Order?"

Lana walked over to him, her face taking on a sad expression, though her eyes remained trained on him like a hawk. "To be honest, he wasn't part of the Order. He didn't want to be. He felt like he could do better on his own, and he had a very, very hard time trusting other people."

"Bad move, Russell, very bad move," Thomas said, shaking his head.

"If he had been a part of the Order, we could have protected him," Lana continued, "and he'd still be alive."

"How could you have protected him from getting killed by the chupacabra?" Clivo asked, confused. "Going after dangerous beasts is pretty much part of the job, isn't it?"

Lana seemed taken aback. "You don't know how he really died, do you?"

Thomas sauntered out of the room. "This is about to get awkward, so I'm going to retire to the kitchen."

Clivo's hair stood up even more. He didn't like where this conversation was going.

Lana squeezed his arm in sympathy, though her nails felt like claws. "Your dad wasn't killed by a chupacabra, Clivo. He was killed by a fellow cryptid catcher."

Clivo's mouth dropped open and his stomach froze. "That's not true."

"I'm so sorry, but it *is* true. The Order tried desperately to protect him, we really did, but he refused our help. Everyone knew that he was the best catcher, and it was just a matter of time before someone from the evil resistance came after him."

Clivo's head was spinning. His father had been *murdered*? He felt a confusing mixture of sadness and anger burning in his chest. "Who killed him?" Clivo could barely get the words out through his tight throat.

Lana sighed, "We actually don't know. There were a lot of people out there who wanted him gone; we just don't know who was able to get to him. But the point is that these same people are going to come after you, and the good guys can't afford to lose another Wren. Please don't make the same mistake your father did. Let us protect you. Join the Order."

Clivo bit back his tears. He was having a hard time focusing on what Lana was saying. He knew he should be asking more questions, prying more into who exactly Lana and Thomas were, but all he could think about was his father.

Lana's quiet voice shook him out of his thoughts. "Clivo? Do you understand how much danger you're in?"

Clivo gripped the edge of his father's desk for support. He wasn't concerned about his own safety anymore; all he could think about was how he didn't want the immortal to ever fall into the hands of the person who had killed his father. But Clivo couldn't ensure that if he was dead himself. "If I joined the Order, how could you protect me?"

Lana smiled patiently. "Like this."

She quickly swung her right arm toward Clivo, who jumped into action and easily blocked it.

He brought his face right up to hers. "Sorry, but you're going to have to do better than that if you want to protect a Wren."

Lana winked at him. "Actually, I haven't started yet."

In a heartbeat, she unleashed a flurry of maneuvers on Clivo. He recognized her throws, traps, clinches, and strikes as something like jujitsu, but she was much stronger and faster than he was. They whirled around the small den, grappling on the rug, finally wrestling themselves into the dining room just as Thomas exited the kitchen.

"Oh boy, chief, did you ask for a demonstration of how she could protect you? She *loves* it when people do that!" Thomas said gleefully.

Clivo began sweating profusely from the effort of defending himself against Lana's relentless attack. In the end, he found himself sprawled on the floor, pinned in a one-armed lock, Lana's other arm pulled back, ready to strike.

"You win!" Clivo exclaimed.

"Is that your safe word?" Lana asked, her breath coming quickly.

"Whatever, just get off me, please," Clivo huffed.

When she had released him he hauled himself to his feet.

Lana stood up as well and pushed a few stray hairs out of her face. "So, to sum up, we'd like you to join the Order because not only are we the good guys, and not only can we protect you, but there's also something else."

"I can hardly wait to hear what it is," Clivo mumbled, straightening his clothes and feeling embarrassed about being fully outfought.

Thomas held up the briefcase and shook the handcuff chain dramatically. "We discovered who the immortal is."

XVI

Clivo stood at the dining room table, the only sound the rattling and banging of the furnace downstairs. He was having a hard time thinking properly. Within an hour he had learned that his father had been killed by a fellow cryptid catcher and that this secret organization he had never heard of knew who the immortal was.

Thomas finally cleared his throat in a dramatic fashion. "A simple thanks for figuring out who the ultimate is would be appropriate here, chief."

"How do you know?" Clivo replied, more sharply than he had intended.

Lana took a seat at the table. "The Order hasn't been wasting time going after every cryptid out there. We've used our time more wisely by focusing on *exactly* which one is the immortal."

"And how do you know someone hasn't already found it?" Clivo asked, remaining standing. "You probably don't even know which cryptids my dad found."

"We don't know that, that's true," Lana explained.

"Your dad was searching for the immortal, but he also wanted to protect the other cryptids, so he never let anyone know which ones he caught. But not everyone is so noble. A legendary creature could fetch a lot of money in a sale to either science or a zoo. If anyone else ever found a cryptid, they'd make sure the whole world knew about it. Most people would do anything for the notoriety, and the money, that came with it. Only the members of the Order have agreed to keep it a secret."

"Speaking of which, chief, how many cryptids did your dad find, anyway?" Thomas asked, taking a seat, kicking his feet up onto the table, and placing the briefcase handcuffed to his wrist on the floor next to him.

"Twelve," Clivo said proudly.

Thomas whistled. "Legendary."

"Do you know how he found them?" Lana asked, a little too casually.

Clivo stared at her. He still didn't trust them, secret order or no. Until he fully did, he knew it was his job to protect the Myth Blasters, and even Douglas, although he wouldn't have minded watching Lana give the cranky old man a good butt kicking. "He worked alone, like I do."

"So how did you find Nessie?" Lana pressed.

Clivo smiled. "After we find the immortal and it's safe from the bad guys, I'll tell you."

Lana narrowed her eyes just a fraction, but moved on.

"Anyway, the Order has been digging through legends and folklore for decades, figuring out which creatures are just stories and which actually exist. But we didn't try to find the cryptids themselves, just things they left behind."

"Like what?" Clivo asked, his interest causing him to take a seat.

"What we all leave behind," Thomas said, picking at his teeth with a fingernail. "Strands of hair. Flakes of skin. Droppings."

"Is that what the lab coat is for? To analyze poop samples?" Clivo asked, not attempting to hide the mockery in his voice.

"Don't knock it, chief, everyone's poop tells a very interesting story." Thomas pulled a bag of nuts from the lab coat's pocket and popped one in his mouth.

Clivo was about to respond but stopped when he saw Lana's eyes shooting daggers at him, so he sank in his seat and motioned for her to continue, which she promptly did.

"Over the years, we haven't found an actual cryptid because we didn't need to waste our time finding every single one. We just needed to find the one that mattered, the immortal. So we examined what they left behind, figuring that if the cryptid was the immortal one, something in its hair or nail samples would indicate so."

Clivo considered that. It all made sense, that was for sure. "So, who's the immortal?"

Thomas kicked his legs off the table and, with a

flourish, laid the briefcase on top, like a magician preparing for his final trick. Lana pulled a key from her pocket and opened the sturdy locks. Clivo tried to peer inside, but Thomas moved the case so he couldn't see anything. Clivo sighed and waited as Thomas slowly pulled out a plastic bag and laid it on the table. Clivo instantly reached for it, but Thomas slapped his hand away.

"No touching, please," Thomas chided.

Clivo rolled his eyes and leaned in for a closer look. Inside the plastic bag was a ball of what looked to be brown fur. "What's that?" Clivo asked.

"A sample." Thomas grinned. "The immortal is none other than the Otterman, otherwise known as the Kooshdakhaa."

"I still have no idea what that is," Clivo replied.

"It's a mythical creature, half man and half otter. Legend says it either saves people from freezing to death or eats small children," Lana explained, applying a fresh coat of red lipstick. "We found that sample in a southeastern Alaska rain forest. It tested as fur belonging to no known animal and—"

"Let me! Let me!" Thomas said, snatching the bag. He carefully pulled out a sample of fur and held it in front of Clivo's face. "Watch this." He grabbed a lighter from his pocket and set fire to the fur, which promptly turned a bright silver and flashed like a sparkling firework. Thomas lowered his voice to a whisper. "All creatures, one blood.

Some remain hidden, others come fore. In one who is hidden, the blood is gone, replaced by the spring of life. A silver lightning drop of eternity."

Clivo let out a laugh of disbelief. "That's your proof? A bit of sparkling fur?"

Thomas threw the fur on the floor in frustration and stomped on it with his foot, leaving a burned spot on the carpet. "What more do you want, chief? We can't drag the Otterman in here and have him confirm it to you personally!"

"The proof is good, Clivo," Lana said, leaning toward him with a glint in her eye. "But even if we've made some kind of mistake, which we haven't, the worst that will happen is you'll cross another cryptid off your list."

"Or it'll eat my face off," Clivo mumbled. He ran a hand through his hair and let out a heavy exhale. "So, I guess you've come to me with this information because you want me to find it?"

Lana smiled. "We're here to help each other. We discovered the immortal; now you need to catch it."

"With our protection of course," Thomas added.

"How are *you* going to protect me?" Clivo asked him. "What skills do you have, besides an unhealthy interest in fur collecting?"

Thomas cracked his knuckles. "That's for me to know and you to find out."

"Time is of the essence, Clivo," Lana continued.

"There's an evil resistance out there searching for the immortal. It's only a matter of time before they find it."

Clivo looked at the bag of fur. Was it possible? Was the Otterman really the immortal? Lana was right, though. Even if it wasn't, it was another cryptid crossed off his list. But if it was, he had to get there before someone from the evil resistance found it. Especially the person who had killed his father. "Come back tomorrow afternoon. I'll try to find out where the Otterman is by then."

"How will you do that?" Lana asked, her eyes once again probing him, as if trying to read his mind.

"Like I said, once the immortal is in safe hands, I'll be happy to tell you."

Clivo waited until Lana and Thomas's rental car was far down the driveway before Skyping Stephanie. With the time change it was probably close to her bedtime, but he hoped she was still awake. It took a few moments, but eventually Stephanie's face appeared on the screen. Clivo knew she was in her room, as evidenced by the large bed behind her and the poster of Stephen Hawking on the wall. She was wearing flannel pajamas, her hair was sloppily pulled back, and she was munching on takeout Chinese food with chopsticks.

"Hi, Stephanie," Clivo said, relieved that she had picked up.